The Hat Pin Murders

Enjoy and God Bless

Joyce Cardel

8/2011

The Hat Pin Murders

Joyce Caudel

Gray Dog Press
Spokane, WA

Gray Dog Press
Spokane, Washington
www.GrayDogPress.com

The Hat Pin Murders
Copyright © 2010 Joyce Caudel
All Rights Reserved

No part of this work may be reproduced or transmitted in any form or by any means, electronic or mechanical, photocopying, recording, or by any information retrieval or storage system without the express written permission of the author.

This is a work of fiction. Names, characters, places, and incidents are the product of the author's imagination or are used fictitiously. Any resemblance to real persons, places, establishments, or locales is entirely coincidental. This book is not a product of the Red Hat Society, and no endorsement or affiliation should be inferred.

While the characters and events portrayed in this novel are fictional, any mention of the Red Hat Society is in reference to one of the largest women's social organizations in the world. The Red Hat Society supports and encourages women to pursue fun, friendship, freedom, fulfillment of lifelong dreams and fitness. If you would like to learn more about the Society or become a Member, please visit the website at www.redhatsociety.com.

ISBN: 978-1-936178-39-1

Printed in the United States of America

I dedicate this book to my mother, Natalie Scaggs, the best mother a girl could have.

"Her children arise up, and call her blessed."
Proverbs 31:28 KJV

Acknowledgement

Sue Ellen Cooper, Exalted Queen Mother of the Red Hat Society, you taught us how to play again and sparked our imaginations into believing we could do anything, even write a novel. To all my Red Hat sisters around the globe, here's to us: CHEERS!

To my husband George, thank you for your love and encouragement. You served as a sounding board and gave me many ideas, you always cheered me on.

To Russ Davis of Gray Dog Press, thank you for taking time to read my manuscript and finally publishing it. You made my dreams come true.

Chapter 1

If Maggie Coppenger had known what horror this day held for her and her friend Mary, she would have crawled back under her fluffy down comforter, buried her head under the pillow and refused to get out of bed. However, Maggie couldn't see into the future, and since she had no idea what lay ahead she plunged into the day with all the gusto of a child going to a birthday party. She hurried through the breakfast dishes, made the bed, and then went to her closet and took out the new dress she had bought especially for today. *I love this dress— it was worth every penny,* she thought as she slipped the dress over her head. Maggie looked into the full length mirror. *Thirty pounds ago, you would have looked terrific in this dress.* She turned sideways, took in a deep breath, patted her stomach, and said, "Oh well, you still look pretty good for an old broad."

At sixty years of age Maggie was still feeling good about life. Her five foot seven inch frame seemed to be holding up well in spite of some arthritis here and there. She noticed that lately her dark brown hair seemed to be glowing with a little silver, but today she would be wearing her red hat so nobody would notice her hair. She slipped her feet into the two-inch-high purple pumps, wishing she could still wear the really high ones that she wore before comfort became more important than style.

Maggie grabbed her hat and purse, and with exaggerated flourish she threw a bright purple feather boa around her neck. She was just walking out of her bedroom when the phone rang.

"Hello, Mary," she giggled into the phone. She knew it would be her friend Mary Reed. Maggie had offered to give her a ride to the gathering; Mary's house was on the way and there was no sense in both of them taking a car.

"Yes, Mary, I'm just about to leave. I'll be at your house in a few minutes." A chuckle escaped her as she hung up the phone. "Oh Mary," she said to herself, "you are excited about today. I'm so glad to see you enjoying life again."

Maggie backed her Ford SUV out of the driveway. The bright sun felt warm through the open sunroof. The sky was clear and blue with huge white fluffy clouds floating along. *What a beautiful day!* she thought as she headed for Mary's house.

Mary lived just a few blocks from Maggie in a cute yellow house with white shutters at the windows. A white picket fence surrounded the yard, giving the place a charming atmosphere. A yard care company came every week to mow and manicure the lawn, keeping it green and lush. Her roses were the envy of the neighborhood and she loved sharing them with her neighbors. Of course she always had a bouquet on her own dining room table: pink, red, white, or yellow, and sometimes she would mix them.

When the roses were blooming Mary made bouquets, but the harsh Eastern Washington winters didn't allow for flowers in Mary's garden, so during those months she would buy roses at the store. They didn't have the delicious fragrances she loved so much, but they were still beautiful and Mary loved a beautiful rose. Every spring she would find another spot in her yard that needed a rose. Her back yard was as close to an English cottage garden as anyone could want.

Just as Maggie pulled up to the curb in front of her house, Mary stepped out of the front door. "You look like a million!" Maggie said as Mary opened the passenger's door and pulled herself up onto the seat of the SUV. Mary, a petite woman of sixty, was wearing a bright purple silk pants outfit. Fringe edged the sleeves and the hem of her blouse. A rhinestone hatpin was the only decoration on the red beret that sat atop her meticulously groomed white hair.

"Maggie, you're wearing that beautiful new dress. It is so elegant and you look great in it. We'll have to go shopping together more often. I'm glad you talked me into this pantsuit, it's so comfortable and the material feels so luscious." Mary hunched her shoulders as she rubbed her hands up and down her arms in a little self-hug.

"If it had been in my size I'd have bought it for myself," Maggie said.

"Where's your hat?" Mary asked.

"Oh, don't worry about that, it's on the back seat. I'll put it on when we get there. I couldn't show up at the most important Red Hat event of the year without my red hat!"

The neighborhood seemed to come alive now that spring had arrived. Mary waved to a neighbor who was working in his yard. A few others were standing in a driveway discussing whatever it is that neighbors discuss on a beautiful Saturday morning.

"Oh look, Maggie, there goes Edith with her dog. She's such a little thing and that dog just pulls her along. It's fun to watch, just waiting for the dog to take off and drag her down the street." Suddenly Mary slapped her mouth. "Oh, forgive me, I shouldn't say such things. Nothing good ever comes from that kind of talk."

"Nothing good will come to Edith after the way she treats her neighbors and especially you. There's no excuse for the way she treated you." Maggie took note that several people seemed to step away as Edith and her dog walked past.

"Yes, it really scared me, but she hasn't bothered me since that last incident."

"Mary, you really should have reported her and her dog to the police. When a person's life is threatened the police should know about it."

"It was just a stupid thing, her dog digging up my roses. All I wanted was for her to keep her dog in her own yard. She acted like it was my fault her dog dug under my fence and tore up some of my roses. She was even mad at me because he tracked mud on her carpet when he went home."

"And she pushed you and threatened to do you harm. It's unbelievable. She has a real mental problem and if she ever threatens you again I insist you file a police report."

"I just stay clear of her. I don't think she will be a problem again. Her daughter came over and apologized. She said Edith was off her meds."

"That's a likely story. When anyone does something stupid, they use that as an excuse, because they are off their meds. Then for her to say those hateful things about our Red Hat club. That really burns me up."

"We love our Red Hat club," Mary exclaimed as she pounded her fist on the armrest. "I don't care what Edith says. What does she know, anyway? She doesn't seem to have any fun. She's always so grumpy."

"Forget about her, Mary, we're going to have fun today."

"I woke up early this morning and could hardly wait for you to come pick me up."

Mary was as happy and excited as Maggie had seen her in a long time.

"Maggie, have you talked to the other gals? Will they all be there? I got Becky a new pink hat and a lavender sweater, hoping she would like to come too, but I don't expect to see her there. You know how young girls are, always busy."

"Becky's just not mature enough to have fun yet. That's why we put those young gals in pink hats. How is she doing, anyway?"

"She's always wishing she had money for all the finer things in life. I try to do all I can for her. I take her shopping for nice clothes and shoes. I told her I would help her with tuition if she would go to college. She has a bright mind and I think she could do most anything she wanted but she has such a rebellious spirit. I keep praying for her. I told her she will never be able to have all the things she wants if she doesn't do something with her life."

"Maybe she thinks she'll marry a rich man." Maggie smiled sheepishly. "That was always my dream as a girl."

"The young ones don't usually come with money, though. I love her like a daughter, Maggie. I'd do anything I could to help her."

"You grew up poor and you turned out all right and you didn't have a sweet aunt to help you out," Maggie said. "And you're right—she needs to put some positive effort into her life."

Mary had no children of her own. She had a stepdaughter, Darlene, but was never able to get close to her because Darlene resented Mary for marrying her father. Darlene's parents had been divorced for several years before Mary and Hank even met. Darlene was very young when her parents divorced. Still, she accused Mary of breaking up her parents' marriage.

"Becky and Darlene hang around together. She tries to keep up with Darlene, who has a trust fund Hank left her, and of course her mother's family has money so Darlene never wants for anything. She's the typical rich kid. Sometimes I think Darlene hangs around with Becky so she can feel superior."

"Let's not talk about kids today. Cheer up, Mary. This is supposed to be fun."

"You're right, I want to think about old friends and good times," Mary said as she clapped her hands together, causing her charm bracelet to make a jingling sound.

Maggie pulled onto the highway, leaving behind their little residential community. Winter snow had melted and the spring rain had caused weeds and wildflowers to grow thick.

Tall pine trees lining the road were lush and green, thriving on the cold Eastern Washington winter that had just passed.

"Isn't it beautiful?" Maggie said. "We really have it all here: spring, summer, fall, and winter. We have all four seasons, and just look at that sky, so clear and blue. So far the smog hasn't gotten this far north."

"I love it here too, although I've never traveled so I don't know what other places are like. But I'm quite content right here in Sommer, tending my roses."

"We do have a harsh winter now and then, but our summers are almost perfect, not too hot. The humidity in some other places is downright unbearable. Besides, the traffic's not bad and the pace is just right for us old folks." Maggie laughed remembering her last trip to California.

The two women chatted about the Red Hat gathering they were about to attend, speculating about who would be there and what the hotel would serve for brunch. "We'll let the valet park for us," Maggie said as she pulled the big Expedition into the hotel's parking garage. "They always have a nice young man who needs some extra tip money and I love taking in all the luxury of this place." Maggie switched off the engine and handed the keys to the young man as he opened the door for her. At the same time another young man opened the passenger side door and took Mary's hand. As she slid out of the seat the young man noticed that she was very short.

"Allow me," he said as he put both hands around her waist and lifted her down.

"Oh my! Oh my!" Mary gasped, blushed, then smiled broadly. "Thank you."

"My pleasure," the young man said.

Maggie rescued her hat from the back seat. Viewing their reflection in the glass doors as they entered the hotel caused Maggie to burst out laughing. "Just making a statement," she said under her breath.

Mary gasped when she saw the hat Maggie had placed on her head. That it was quite large was an understatement. A veil of red lace and an explosion of red ostrich feathers swept over the silk-covered brim. The lace formed a large bow, then flowed gently down Maggie's back, ending just below her waist.

"Maggie! When did you get that hat? Just wait until Rita sees it. I think you've outdone her this time."

"I hope so. I decorated it to go with this dress and I still have blisters from the hot glue gun. If Rita outdoes me this time I'll give up."

"I can hardly wait to see her face," Mary snickered.

The ladies walked into the elegant lobby of the Sommerset Hotel feeling quite elegant themselves. The Sommerset Hotel was built at the turn of the century. Presidents and royalty had dined and danced there over the years. The evidence was displayed in elaborately framed photos that hung on the museum-quality gilded walls of the elegantly restored hotel. Maggie had had lunch there before and it was wonderful, but this event was to be held in the grand ballroom.

"That was a nice young man," Mary said. "It's been a long time since a handsome young man held my hand and helped me out of a car." As they stepped into the large lobby, Mary stopped walking so she could take in the entire room. "This entrance is breathtaking. I can hardly wait to see the rest of it."

A huge fountain was the focal point in the center of the room. It had three large bowls that caught the water flowing down from one bowl to the next. The sound of flowing water cascading gently down gave a peaceful, relaxing sound that made the ladies want to linger for a while.

Growing up poor, Mary had dreamed of such places. Her dreams came from the books she read, castles and mansions where rich people lived, some fiction and some real but nothing like this. This was a genuine mansion. Even on this warm spring day there was a fire in the massive fireplace. As Mary walked the full length of the room she stretched out her hands to feel the warmth of the fire.

"Hank would have loved it here, if only he hadn't got sick, if only he had lived." In a second Mary was transported back to their honeymoon. After their simple wedding ceremony with Mary's brother Paul and his wife Ellie as their witnesses, Hank and Mary had made the three-hour drive to Leavenworth, Washington. Mary couldn't remember much about the drive except that she was with the man she loved. They stayed in a little inn at the foot of the mountains in the quaint Bavarian village. She was sure it was the most wonderful three-day honeymoon anyone ever had. They went into all the little shops buying souvenir trinkets that Mary still treasured. Hank was so handsome, they were so young and in love, they thought it would go on forever.

"Isn't it beautiful, Mary? It's perfect for a romantic getaway; maybe I'll get Frank to bring me here for our anniversary." Maggie sat down on one of the beautifully upholstered chairs. "Did you hear me? Hey girlfriend, come back from wherever you are."

Mary jerked as if she had been sleeping. "Sorry, I was just thinking about Hank, wishing he could be here. Yes, it's better than I imagined—marble floors, looks like gold everywhere, and the lovely flower arrangements. Why don't we just spend the whole weekend here?"

Maggie laughed. "They're probably booked full. I hear you have to make reservations months in advance and I don't think they allow sleeping on their beautiful sofas."

A pretty young woman wearing a burgundy suit and a nametag that read "Ann–Hostess" suddenly appeared next to Mary. "Are you here for the Red Hat gathering?"

"Yes, thank you, we are part of the Red Hats," Maggie said.

The sudden appearance of the hostess startled Mary.

"This place is so lovely, you must love working here," she said.

"Yes, it is lovely, isn't it? My name's Ann. If I can be of assistance just let me know. I see you all have nametags, too."

"Yes, I'm Mary Reed. This is my friend Maggie Coppenger. We're part of the Mystery Mamas."

"I love that! How did you come up with that name?" Ann asked.

"We meet every week to discuss a book we are reading. It's always a mystery, so Mystery Mamas," Mary told her.

"I like it. Well, if there is anything I can do for you, let me know. The Red Hats are on the second floor. You can take the escalator." Ann pointed toward the escalator then turned and walked away.

Mary's eyes followed the hostess back to the door marked Office. "What a pleasant young lady."

"Yes," Maggie said as she watched the hostess walk away. "Very pleasant."

"Young people aren't usually so friendly. The Sommerset Hotel must have high standards for their employees," Mary said.

Just then Mary spotted her stepdaughter, Darlene, coming down the steps from the restaurant with her mother.

"Darlene, Janet, hello," Mary said as she walked toward them. "How nice to see you. This is my friend Maggie. We're here for the Red Hat gathering."

Maggie smiled and stepped forward.

"Hello, Mary, how nice. We're on our way out. Have a nice day," Janet said as they hurried away.

"Ciao," Darlene said and gave a little wave as she walked past, ignoring Maggie.

Maggie's heart ached for Mary. Mary tried so hard to be friends with Darlene, only to have her feelings hurt with each encounter. "Come on Mary, we're here to have a good time. Let's show off our new outfits and have some fun."

The escalator was built to resemble an elegant staircase with carved wooden handrails that curved up to the second floor. As Maggie and Mary stepped off the escalator, Mary said, "That was a nice ride. I'd be out of breath if I had to climb the stairs up here."

"This was a real staircase when this place was first built. This was the place to be seen in those days. Can you imagine the elegantly dressed ladies and gentlemen in their tuxedoes…?"

"And the children," Mary interrupted. "Little girls in their fancy dresses with their hair in long curls. Little boys in short pants with their hair slicked down."

"Always the teacher, Mary, that's what I love about you," Maggie told her.

"Speaking of elegantly dressed ladies, just look at us, Maggie. Let's go inside and join the fun."

The chatter of many women greeted them as they entered the ballroom. The whole area was a maze of purple and red. Although they had arrived early there was already a large crowd gathered.

"Maggie, look, there's Susan and Jessica. Oh my goodness don't they both look great, but look at Susan's hat! I love it and she looks so chic in her purple and gold caftan."

Susan's hat had a large brim that was surrounded by bright red silk roses and a big silk bow. Two large red ostrich plumes jetted out from behind the bow, and she wore the hat tilted a little to one side. Maggie was delighted to see that Susan was able to get a new hat for the occasion. "Susan! Your hat is incredible. Where did you get it?"

Susan whispered in Maggie's ear. "It's that old one that I've worn a dozen times, just added a few new flowers and feathers to jazz it up a bit."

"They certainly did the trick," Maggie whispered back. Then more loudly she said, "You look the part of the title we bestowed upon you. Duchess Susan of Mystery certainly fits you now." Maggie gave a little curtsy. "Duchess Susan by your leave?"

Jessica greeted both ladies with a tip of their hats. "Here's a name tag for each of you. We found our seats. We are right up front, a perfect spot. There was a reserved sign on the table with our chapter name on it."

"Rita does take care of us," Susan said.

"Don't you just love this place?" Mary touched the linen table cloth. "I could have brunch here every day."

"Not at the price we had to pay for today's brunch," Susan said. "This is my limit for the month, but I guess I can afford to splurge once in a while, especially when I'm with my best friends. I'm glad we could all come. And, don't we all look marvelous? We have to have someone take our picture."

"Yes, we look so smart all dressed up in our purple outfits and red hats. I'm surprised with all these feathers we aren't having allergy attacks," Mary said as she faked a sneeze. "I have never had so much fun as I have since we joined the Red Hats."

"Mary, if you have to be over fifty—"

"Over fifty!" Mary interrupted. "Some of these ladies are eighty and ninety years young and still going strong!"

"All right, Mary, whatever your age, you had best have fun doing it," Susan said, giving her friend a hug. "I'm having the time of my life, too. Here's our table, isn't everything beautiful? Come on, let's do some mingling."

The ladies all set off in different directions as they spotted old friends in the crowd. Mary found her dear friend and fellow teacher, Alice Hastings. Alice was still teaching at the elementary school and filled Mary in on all the latest happenings there.

"I miss the children, Alice. I have a lot of time on my hands. I would love to do some volunteer work at the school. I know there are children needing some extra attention, especially the slow readers. I could go in a couple times a week," Mary said.

"Mary, that would be wonderful. There are two in my class that could use some extra help. Surely there are more in the other classes." Alice smiled. The thought of getting some extra help in the classroom was very welcome.

"I know there's never enough time in the day to give all the children the attention they need. I'll call the principal first thing Monday morning."

"The new principal is a great guy, Mary. He's easygoing and really has a handle on the kids. I know he will be thrilled to meet you."

"Thanks, Alice. I'm really excited about this. Well, I'd better scoot, good to see you."

Mary missed the children. She had taught fourth grade for many years. She thought it was the perfect time in a child's life. They were so teachable, so eager to learn.

She needed to keep busy. She had plenty of time on her hands and what better way to spend it than working with children. Mary's thoughts were filled with possibilities. She would take it slow, two mornings a week for a couple of hours. *When I get excited about something I tend to go overboard,* Mary thought. *Pace yourself now, remember you're retired.* Mary had such sweet memories of teaching at the school where her husband Hank was the principal—it was all so perfect. *Hank, why did you have to die? We could be spending our golden years together. Traveling, being together, we were so happy. Now all I have are these crazy Red Hat ladies. Maggie saved my life, Hank. After you died, Maggie was there for me. She helped me realize my life wasn't over and I need to live it to the fullest. I'm going to relish life, every minute I have left. I'm going to start reading with kids again. But today I'm enjoying this beautiful place. I'm going to stuff myself with good food, spend time with good friends and have a blast.* Mary spotted another acquaintance, got her attention, and headed her way.

Maggie found Rita Johnson, the Queen Bee. She was called that by most of the Red Hat ladies, because she was the one who organized these gatherings. Rita sent invitations to all the Red Hat groups and kept them informed as to what was going on in the area. She had organized today's program and found vendors who would set up their sales booths, selling any number of things pertaining to the Red Hat theme.

"Rita, I've been looking for you. I want to thank you for all your hard work. Everything is wonderful, so elegant! Did you have help from the hotel staff?"

Rita, a stunningly beautiful woman, at five feet ten inches tall looked like a fashion model in her royal colors. Her red wool fedora, graced with red feathers and a large diamond brooch, sat on top of her long blond hair. She was draped in diamonds from her ears to her toes. Maggie knew they were only cubic zirconium but so what, she looked fabulous. Her high-heeled sandals gave her a height of over six feet. The purple satin dress she wore clung just tight enough to show off her hourglass figure. Over one shoulder she draped a long, purple marabou boa.

"Maggie, it's good to see you. Let me look at that hat," Rita said as she slowly circled her friend. "You've done it, you've captured the Red Hat spirit! That is the most incredible hat I've ever seen. I give up. I'll never be able to outdo you with this one."

"Good," Maggie said. "I finally put my imagination to work and this is what I came up with. I'm glad you like it. Anyway, I hope the hotel staff set this all up. You didn't call me to help you."

"Yes, I just told them what we wanted and they set everything up. It is perfect isn't it? Of course we are paying for it with the cost of the brunch, and the vendors are paying for a spot to sell their goodies. But these ladies expect to be able to purchase Red Hat items while they're here. Did you check out Lady Diane's hat booth?" Rita swooned.

"Don't tempt me, but yes I stopped by her booth and I have my eye on one of her purple hats."

"That's right, you and Frank have an anniversary coming up. You can wear a purple hat for your anniversary or birthday! Great idea, Maggie. After all, shopping is our official sport," Rita said.

"I need some new earrings and I think I spotted just what I've been looking for. Spread the wealth around, I always say." Maggie started toward the jewelry vendor when Rita grabbed her arm and pulled her back.

"Maggie, keep an eye out. There's a young lady, blond, very pretty but no one seems to know her. She's acting a little strange. I've had a few gals ask about her. She has on a purple sweater and a red hat but she's awfully young for red. The girls that have talked to her said she doesn't seem to know anything about the Red Hats, but she's a sweet person. She doesn't stay around long enough to get acquainted. She keeps going into the bar talking to some guy there."

"A purple sweater, red hat… Yes, Rita, she should be easy to spot."

"I know, but some of the ladies are concerned."

"Well, what is the problem and what am I supposed to do with her if I find her?" Maggie wanted to know. "Maybe she's had too much to drink. Maybe the guy brought her here and is waiting to take her home. We should find out what group she belongs to."

"I haven't seen her up close but from what several of the gals have said, she doesn't seem old enough for red and if she was part of a group, they'd have her in pink. When asked which group she belongs to she just says she's a Red Hatter, then gets up and moves away. I don't think she bought a ticket, at least she hasn't been eating. Oh well, anyway, Maggie, if you see her, see what you can find out. I've got to mingle now. Oh, by the way, I'm going to need your help planning our next event, so be prepared," Rita said as she walked away. She saw the mystery woman and started after her, but once again she moved out of sight. Rita stopped, tried to get her bearings and decide if she should go into the bar to speak to the man the mystery woman seemed to know. Just then she was distracted by a little white-haired lady looking for the restroom. Rita pointed her in the right direction, then she headed for the jewelry vendors.

Maggie purchased a pair of earrings from one of the vendors. As she turned to walk away she almost bumped into a woman in a flowing lavender chiffon gown. Her huge brimmed hat was made of soft pink chiffon.

"Well as I live and breathe, if it isn't Maggie Coppenger. Woodward just hasn't been the same since you left."

"Loraine Stapleton, how are you? How is Abby? I think of her so often."

Abby Stapleton had been one of Maggie's favorite children at the boarding school where she served as dean of girls for over twenty years. Abby's parents, Hershel and Loraine Stapleton, had money and wanted their daughter to have every advantage, which simply meant anything Abby wanted Abby got. *Just keep her happy and out of our hair.* Hershel Stapleton, a high-powered attorney with political ties all the way to the White House, was so busy Abby rarely saw him. Her mother, Loraine, was more concerned with her standing in the social register than with her daughter. *Besides, isn't that why they paid the outrageous tuition?*

Loraine Stapleton was wearing a diamond necklace. Maggie was certain it was the real thing. She also wore her famous five-carat solitaire. It was made famous around Woodward School by her daughter Abby. More than once Abby had tried to impress the other girls with stories about her mother's diamond collection.

"Abby is just a handful. You were the only one that fully appreciated her eccentricities," Loraine said.

"Well, I put a lot of prayer into the girls at Woodward.

Abby was always very special to me and I still pray for her," Maggie explained.

"I didn't realize you were part of the Red Hats. It was nice seeing you, ciao!" Loraine Stapleton floated off, dismissing Maggie with a wave of her diamond-covered hand.

Maggie heard someone call her name. "Maggie, I thought that was you."

"Milly Good? Milly, it's been years, how nice to see you!"

"Yes, it's been at least two years. Do you know my friend Marie Reader? Marie just joined our Red Hat group."

"Marie, it's nice to meet you. I must confess I thought you were my friend Mary Reed. You look so much alike and your names are so similar."

"It's nice meeting you, Maggie. You will have to introduce me to my other self."

"She's around here somewhere. We'll have to get you two together," Maggie said.

"Marie has a beautiful voice," Milly explained. "She's joined our Singing Sisters group and she's teaching us some dance steps to go with our songs."

"I did a lot of this sort of thing in school, but lately my singing is all done in the church choir. Milly took me under her wing and introduced me to Red Hatting. I'm really enjoying myself."

"That's what it's all about—fun!" Maggie said.

"Marie sang a solo on Sunday; she has a beautiful voice."

"How nice you both attend the same church," Maggie said.

"Yes, and we are neighbors, too," Marie said. "I was a little reluctant when Milly asked me to attend a Red Hat meeting. I'd heard some wild stories about Red Hatters, but I was thrilled to find some real Christian fellowship."

"By the way your outfit is gorgeous!" Maggie said.

"Thank you. I'm really getting into this purple thing. In

just a short time I've accumulated quite a few purple items for my wardrobe."

Milly interrupted. "She makes all her clothes, Maggie. This outfit would cost a small fortune. But Marie whipped it up in a few evenings on her little sewing machine."

"Oh Milly, when you enjoy something it's easy," Marie said.

"It's really nice meeting you, Marie." Maggie smiled. "We'll be seeing a lot of each other at these Red Hat gatherings. I can hardly wait for your next performance."

"Yes, Maggie, let's keep in touch. Say hello to Mary for me," Milly said as she and Marie walked away.

Jessica and Susan had found old friends and were busy talking and admiring hats. "It's like an old-fashioned Easter Parade," Jessica said. "This really takes me back a long time. In my younger days, women used to wear hats and gloves when they went some place. Of course the hats were much more conservative then."

"I remember when all the department stores had hat departments and there were hat boutiques, small stores that specialized in hats," Susan said. "That's why this is so much fun. Then women dressed that way all the time. Why my mother wouldn't be caught dead in church without a hat on. Now we do it just for the fun of it."

"And do it so extravagantly!" Jessica added. "Come on, Susan, we had best get back to our table."

Mary was already in her seat sipping coffee. "The coffee's good and it's piping hot," Mary said. "I saw my old friend Alice Hastings; she's still teaching school. We had a nice chat about old times."

"Pass the coffee, Mary, I need some caffeine," Jessica said, holding her cup for Mary to pour. "You miss the kids, don't you?"

"Yes, I've got too much time on my hands. I'm thinking

about doing some volunteer work at the school. I'll call Monday and get an appointment with the principal."

"Mary, that's a great idea. The kids need all the help they can get these days. Besides, we all need to do our part to make the world a better place, and you are such a positive role model."

"Are you talking about me, Jess?" Maggie asked, slipping into the seat beside her. "I ran into Milly Good."

"Milly, I haven't seen her in ages. How is she?" Mary asked.

"She looks great, as always. She introduced me to a new member of their Singing Sisters group."

"Oh, I love them!" Susan interrupted. "Those gals are so much fun. Their costumes are really cute. Always makes me want to get up and dance."

"As I was saying," Maggie continued, "this new gal. At first I thought she was you, Mary. You could be sisters. Her name is Marie. Sounds like she will be a great addition to their act. She and Milly are neighbors and they attend the same church."

"Listen up, girls, Rita's about to do her thing," Susan interrupted.

Rita Johnson stepped up to the microphone and, using her kazoo, played a little fanfare. "Okay, Hatties, if you will all take your seats we can get started."

The Hatties clapped their hands and some gave toots with their kazoos.

Rita offered up a short prayer. "Now, let's eat!"

The tables were set beautifully, with gold-rimmed china, white linen tablecloths and napkins. The Hatties started passing the muffins and pouring coffee. It seemed everyone was chatting at the same time.

Mary looked up at the ceiling while chewing a bite of her blueberry muffin.

"Did you ever see such a beautiful place? This ballroom is breathtaking."

The domed ceiling of the ballroom looked as if white clouds were floating in a pale blue sky. Cherubs were holding delicately painted flowers intertwined in groups of twos and threes. Chandeliers lit the room and hung like thousands of diamonds cascading out of the clouds. The scene was so peaceful, Mary felt as if she were gazing right into heaven.

* * *

Mary Reed sat on a velvet-covered loveseat just around the corner from the ballroom entrance. On an antique table in front of her was a huge arrangement of blood red roses. Mary knew them by name: Precious Platinum, brilliant in their color, exceptionally hardy, perfect for the climate here in the northwest. But Mary wasn't looking at the roses. She was just sitting there with her red beret a little lopsided on her head. Her white hair, always meticulously groomed, was mussed. Her eyes were fixed, staring into nothing. Her beautiful purple blouse was soaked with her own blood.

Chapter 2

The party was over and Maggie was ready to go home—her feet were killing her. She had given Mary a ride to the gathering so she had to find her. *She's probably in the ladies' room*, Maggie thought. Taking off her shoes, she carried them along with her handbag and a few mementos from the party. The ladies' restroom was beautiful.

There on the counter was a basket of hand towels rolled in neat little bundles. Another basket had small packets of hand lotions and samples of colognes. Gold fixtures and marble counters added to the elegance of the room. The individual toilets were enclosed like little closets. Maggie thought Mary was probably in one of them. She knocked on each door. "Mary, are you in there? I'm ready to go. Mary, answer me!" There was no answer. "She's probably taking a tour of this place, but I'm going to sit for a minute." Maggie sat down on one of the Queen Anne chairs in the lounge and rubbed her feet for a few minutes. As she leaned back in the chair she saw a life-size doll, representing a Red Hat lady, sitting on one of the sofas opposite her. The doll was made from pantyhose. Wrinkles were sewn into its face. It was stuffed with cotton batting and wore a purple dress, a bright red hat, and enormously ugly, dangling red earrings. Maggie thought she remembered seeing the doll at the entrance to the ballroom when they arrived. "Someone must have moved you in here. You're sure cute. I wonder who made you. I don't suppose you've seen Mary? No, I thought not. I'll keep looking, she's bound to turn up soon."

Bewildered, Maggie went back to the ballroom. There were still a few ladies standing around talking, but most every-

The Hat Pin Murders

one had left by now. She walked around the large room hoping to find her friend among the small groups of chatting women.

Loraine Stapleton called out, "Maggie, can you help me? I think this place would be perfect for our New Year's Eve party. Hershel wants to impress his clients and I think this would do nicely. You're so good at these things."

"Loraine, I'm just here with the Red Hats. I don't know anything about this place. Rita made all the arrangements. I just need to find my friend Mary so I can take my tired feet home."

"Rita made all the arrangements? There she is." Loraine headed toward Rita with her chiffon gown flowing as she walked. "Rita, oh Rita!"

"Good grief," Maggie said to herself. "That woman! Poor Rita. Well, better her than me. I've got to find Mary." Maggie left the ballroom and walked to a little alcove just around the corner. Beautifully upholstered chairs, loveseats, and a sofa were arranged in a cozy conversation area. Blood red roses floated in a huge glass bowl that sat in the center of an ornately carved antique table.

"Mary, there you are. I've been looking all over for you. Of course I'd find you in a cozy little place like this with a big bowl of roses in front of you. You always manage to find the roses, don't you? I'm ready to leave, how about you?" Maggie sat down on the loveseat next to her friend. "Mary, are you all right?" Maggie reached over and touched Mary's arm. She didn't respond. She was cold. Maggie shook her. She patted her hand. "Mary, wake up! Mary?"

Maggie's eyes went from Mary's face to the beautiful purple blouse she wore. A stain, dark and wet, drew Maggie's fingers to it. It felt thick and sticky, sending impulses from her fingertips to her stomach. Her stomach started wrenching. Cold chills ran down her spine. "Mary?" Maggie placed her hand on her friend's cheek and turned her head. Mary's eyes looked straight into Maggie's but saw nothing. Maggie's hand slipped down the side of Mary's neck where the blood was still thick and wet. "Oh Mary, what happened to you?" A cruel dark presence surrounded Maggie. She couldn't breath. Gasping for air, she slumped to the floor beside her friend, helpless. Maggie felt her mind whirl; she was spinning out of control. Down, down, she was falling, she couldn't help herself. The blackness was swallowing her, deeper and deeper she fell until the blackness swallowed her completely.

* * *

Mary and Maggie had been friends from their first day in kindergarten. Mary lived in the country and rode the bus to school. Maggie lived just a few blocks away, so she walked to school with several kids from the neighborhood. She would wait in front of the school until the bus arrived, and then the two girls would walk into the building hand in hand. They were known on the playground as the M and M twins. In class they were the brightest students, always getting As, the first to raise their hands when the teacher asked a question. It was the same through middle school and high school.

Mary became a teacher and began teaching at the same school she had attended as a child. She thought all her dreams had come true when she married Hank Reed. They were head over heels in love. After Hank's death of a sudden heart attack, Mary seemed to lose interest in everything. Soon after his death she retired from teaching. She was living from day to day, just going through the motions with no goal in mind for the rest of her life. She was lonely and miserable. Then one day her good friend Maggie came over and said, "Mary, I've had enough of you feeling sorry for yourself. I've brought you a gift. It's a red hat. We are going out to lunch." After that luncheon, Mary and Maggie kept a very busy schedule: luncheons, teas, shopping, and their Mystery Readers club.

The Mystery Readers club was a small group of very close friends: Maggie Coppenger, Mary Reed, Jessica Wyatt, Susan Moore, Lisa Scott and Rita Johnson. Their favorite thing to do, when they were not dressing up in their Red Hat finery, was to read mysteries. They met on Monday mornings for coffee to discuss the books they were reading. Usually they would all read a different book. Then when one of them finished reading a book they would pass it on to one of the other gals. They had some lively discussions, but Mary was always impatient to read each book that was being discussed.

"They're all so interesting. I want to read every book that's being discussed and you won't give them up before you finish reading them," Mary said. "I get so frustrated."

"So let's all read the same book, and then we can discuss it together. I know how Mary feels," Jessica said. "By the time one of you finishes the book you're reading, someone else has talked about another one and I'm dying to read it."

"Me too," Susan agreed. "That would solve a lot of my frustration and I think we could have some really good discussions if we were all reading the same book. We could assign a certain number of chapters and we would all be ready for the discussions when we have our weekly meeting."

"We could still get in some extra reading on our own," Maggie chimed in. "As it is I always have at least two books going at the same time."

"I like the idea," Lisa said. That way we can dissect the characters and really get into their motivation."

"Great idea!" Rita said. "Let's take a trip to the mall right now and choose a book. We all seem to like the same kind of mystery so it should work out just fine. I've got time now; if you can all go now, I'll drive."

"I'm ready for a new book," Jessica said.

"I've got nothing else to do. I'm ready if the rest of you are," Lisa said.

Mary nodded her head in agreement.

"Archie's working at the hardware and won't be home until late so count me in," Susan said as she picked up her purse from behind her chair.

"Okay, I guess we're all ready. Frank's at some car club thing. I'll get my purse and let's go," Maggie said.

They all went outside and piled into Rita's big Cadillac to head for the mall.

"Seat belts," Rita said. "This baby doesn't move until everyone's belted in."

"Rita, I love this car, it's sure roomy inside," Lisa said as she clicked her seatbelt.

"You bought it new, didn't you? Seems like you've had it as long as I can remember," Jessica said.

"My dad bought it new for my mother, Elvis pink! They decided to give it to me but I had to promise Mom I'd keep it or give it back to her."

"Wow, that's really special!" Susan said. "It still looks like new."

"Dad comes by on a regular basis and checks on the car, makes sure the oil's changed, stuff like that. He's restored a lot of it over the years as things wear out."

"These classic cars have a way of becoming family members." Maggie rolled her eyes and added, "I think Frank loves his Mustang more than he loves me."

"Oh no, Maggie, the way Frank looks at you, anyone would think he's a lovesick puppy. You two are the envy of every married couple I know," Susan told her.

Maggie, blushing, said, "You're right, Frank and I are still madly in love. Oh, here we are, Rita. Hope you all brought your reading glasses."

Rita pulled into the parking garage.

"There's one on the right, Rita, I think those people are about to back out."

"I see it, Jess. This is a great spot and wide enough for my big boat of a car." Rita eased into the parking spot, put the car in park, set the brake, and turned off the ignition.

The ladies all slid out of the car and Rita locked the doors. Once inside they all headed for the mystery section.

"I love to browse this bookstore. I could spend hours here. If I had to spend the rest of my life in one place it would be in a bookstore," Jessica swooned.

"I'm with you, Jess," Maggie agreed. "Books are a passion with me, too."

"I probably should be reading something more serious, but I just love mysteries," Jessica said. "There sure are a lot to choose from."

"Here's a series where a cat is a detective, and there are mysteries for dog lovers, caterers, hairdressers, it goes on and on," Maggie said.

"I think it's great. No matter what your interest, there is a detective, whether amateur or professional, that will solve the mystery for you," Jessica added.

"I'm trying to read as many of these books as I can. If I read one a day I'll still never read them all." Maggie laughed.

"Well let's get started then," Jessica demanded. "Oh, here's Dorothy Gilman—I love her Mrs. Pollifax series, but I've read every one of them."

"Me too, they are all filled with action and humor. When I grow up I want to be just like Mrs. Pollifax."

"Oh, you are, you just need to learn a little karate," Jessica told her.

"Enough of that, Jess, let's get our books and a latte and sit down and make a decision," Maggie suggested.

After browsing the bookshelves they all decided on Sue Grafton's latest book. Rita took Mary's arm. "Let's see if the store has enough copies to go around."

Mary placed the book on the counter and spoke to the

clerk. "Do you have six copies of this book in stock?"

"Yes, we need six copies," Susan demanded. "One for each of us!"

The clerk went to work on her computer. "Looks like you're in luck; I'll check the storeroom."

Maggie, Jessica, and Lisa were still busy browsing the books. "Oh," Lisa swooned. "Look, look, this place is just full of good reading."

The clerk came back with six copies of the book they had chosen.

Once in the car, the ladies began to talk about the book they had just bought.

"How about that Kinsey Millhoun? Sue Grafton writes about her like she's a real person," Susan said.

"Oh yes, Conan Doyle made Holmes so real he couldn't stand the man," Rita mused. "But he had to live with him for a good many years. He even tried to kill him off once."

"Well *a* to *z* will take a good many years, too, so I hope she is happy with her creation," Lisa said.

"Yes, let's hope she doesn't kill her off in this one," Mary agreed. "I've read all her books to this point and I'd like to read the rest. Finish the alphabet, Sue!"

"No, she can't kill her off yet, she's got a good thing going and she can't leave us hanging," Maggie said.

"This is going to be fun. Let's try to read at least the first three chapters by next week. We will meet at my house," Jessica said. "I've got a new dessert I want to try out on you."

"You always use us as your guinea pigs, Jess," Susan said.

"Well who else can I try things out on, if not my best friends? It's only after you approve it that I can fix it for my son-in-law."

Rita looked in the rearview mirror at Jessica. "I'm always happy to help out. I'll test your desserts any time."

"Rita, how do you stay so slim and trim? You're always

eating and you're the only person I know that never talks about dieting and exercising," Maggie said.

"Good genes, that's all I can tell you. Good genes."

Chapter 3

Maggie tried to open her eyes. Her eyelids were heavy; she couldn't lift them.

Her mind wasn't working either. She was fighting to get through thick black cobwebs. Something was terribly wrong. "Mary?" The blackness engulfed her mind, she was fighting to get through it. "Mary?" Maggie finally opened her eyes. She stared at her bloody hands and began rocking back and forth, unaware of the moaning sound coming from deep within her. Only then did she remember Mary's blank eyes staring at her. Maggie didn't think she would be able to stand. Feeling weak and sick, she just sat there on the floor at Mary's feet.

Ann, the hostess from downstairs, suddenly appeared. "What's going on?" she yelled. "Are you all right? I heard someone yelling for help."

"It's my friend Mary. I just found her like this, she's hurt. Please go call for help!"

Ann stepped closer to the two women. "Hurt? She looks like she's dead to me. You stay right there, I'm going to call the police!"

"Hurry, please hurry," Maggie said. "Please get to a phone and call 911."

Ann took the moving stairs two at a time. Once inside the office she used the phone to dial 911.

"911, what is your emergency?"

Ann yelled breathlessly into the phone. "There's a woman with blood all over her and another woman that looks like she's dead. I'm scared. I really am scared. Please send the police right away." Ann locked herself in the office and waited for the police to arrive.

In just a few minutes two uniformed police officers knocked on the office door. "Did you call about a death and someone with blood all over them?"

"This way, officers, I'll show you where the body is. I hope that woman is still there. She had blood all over her," Ann told them.

As the police officers stepped off the escalator they spotted Maggie. She was still sitting on the floor beside Mary. Her eyes were red and swollen.

One of the officers asked, "What happened here?" He stood like a tower over Maggie, his stern gruff voice demanding, "I said, what happened here!"

"I just found her like this! I don't know what happened! Why is there blood all over her?" Maggie whispered.

"I can see the blood. I see blood on you, too. What's your name?" He helped Maggie to her feet and walked her back a few steps from Mary. "I said, what's your name?"

"I'm Margaret Coppenger," she sobbed. "I think she's dead, she's so cold and all that blood. I need to sit down. I don't feel too good." Maggie's head was spinning. She closed her eyes and hoped this was all a bad dream. If she could just lay down, sleep would make it all go away. Someone brought a chair for her to sit on.

The officer had his notebook out and was writing in it. "Go ahead and tell me what happened. Just start from the beginning."

"I don't feel good. Do we have to do this now?"

"Yes, lady, we have to do this now!"

Maggie tried to control herself. She knew it was important to give as much detail as she could while it was fresh in her mind but since she really didn't know what happened it was all so confusing. "Mary's my friend." She rubbed her hands together, trying to rub off the blood. "I don't know what happened."

"You said you found her this way or did you kill her? Is that how you got the blood on your hands?" the officer grilled.

"No! I didn't kill her, she's my friend," Maggie cried.

"Lady, it looks mighty suspicious, you sitting there with blood all over you. You'll tell me what happened here or you can tell me down at the station."

"She was so cold and blood, all the blood! I yelled for someone to call 911." Maggie felt like she might faint again. "Someone did this to my friend, not me, I'd never hurt Mary. She's dead isn't she?"

"We'll let the medical examiner decide that when he gets here," the policeman said.

The paramedics had arrived and were examining Mary. They seemed to be huddled over her so Maggie couldn't see what they were doing. Finally one of the paramedics stood up and walked over to the officer. He turned his back to Maggie. "She's dead, but the medical examiner will have to make it official. We put the heart monitor on her and got nothing. The blood seems to have come from a puncture wound in her neck. The medical examiner will be able to figure out what happened. We'll call him, we're through here." He nodded toward Maggie. "Do you want us to check her out? She seems pretty upset."

"Yeah, you better check her out. She's gonna have to answer a lot of questions," the officer said.

The paramedic went to Maggie. "I think I had better check you out, you've had quite a shock." He took Maggie's pulse and blood pressure. He watched her for a few minutes. "I think you're okay, just take it easy, take some deep breaths. We can take you to the hospital; it might be a good idea to have a doctor check you out."

"I'll be all right but I'll ride along with Mary. I don't want her to go alone," Maggie said.

"I'm sorry, that's not possible. The coroner will be taking

her body to the morgue. They won't let you go with them," the paramedic explained.

"The morgue, then she's dead, isn't she? She's really dead." Maggie sighed.

"Yes, I'm afraid she's dead," the paramedic said. "You should call your doctor; he can give you something for your nerves. You might want to think about some grief counseling, too."

"Thanks," Maggie said. "It was such a shock, to find her like that."

"The lieutenant's here," one of the officers said. Everyone seemed to snap to attention when the lieutenant came on the scene. "What do you think we oughta do, lieutenant? Most of the people left before we got here. I understand there were about two hundred ladies here," the young officer told him. "All dressed up fit to kill, if you'll pardon the expression, having some kind of tea party. They call themselves Red Hats."

Lieutenant Ron Waters got down on one knee beside Mary's body. He recognized Mary as the little white-haired lady that lived just down the street from him. "Get statements from anyone that's still here. Just do the best you can. Who found her? Get the lab guys up here."

"Ron, oh Ron, I'm so glad it's you!" Maggie rushed over to the lieutenant.

"Maggie? What are you doing here?"

"It's Mary Reed, you know Mary—she lives just down the street. This officer is trying to accuse me of murdering her!"

"Sit down over here, Maggie, and tell me what you were doing here. Do you know what happened?"

Maggie started sobbing again. Ron put his arm around her and sent one of the uniformed officers for a glass of water. Maggie was like a second mother to Ron and his wife Nancy. They had lived next door to each other for fifteen years and were more like family than just neighbors. Maggie had been so proud the day Ron told her that he had made lieutenant and was in charge of the homicide division. Maggie had invited the whole neighborhood to a party to celebrate the occasion. Now they were both remembering how Mary had said that all the ladies in the neighborhood could rest easy with Ron on the job.

Ron Waters was six feet two inches tall, a hundred and ninety pounds, and was ruggedly good looking, with dark brown wavy hair and deep blue eyes. He was soft spoken and gentle with those he cared about. A twenty-year veteran of the police force, he had earned the respect and admiration of everyone he'd ever worked with.

"He's a no-nonsense cop and doesn't put up with any guff from the bad guys. Don't worry, Ms. Coppenger, the lieutenant will find whoever did this terrible thing," the young officer said as he handed Maggie a glass of water and a box of tissues.

"I know," Maggie said. "Ron won't rest until he finds the person that did this." Maggie tried to get control of herself so she could tell Ron what she remembered. "Can I go home now?" Maggie asked.

"Are you all right?" Ron asked. "I can't impress on you how serious this is. It doesn't look very good for you. If I didn't know you like I do I would have to hold you for questioning."

"I know, the other officer made that clear to me. I just want to go home."

"I'll have an officer drive you. I'll be by later."

"My car is in the garage here. I don't want to leave it."

"I'll drive it home for you. I came in a police car. Give me your claim ticket. I'll bring it to you when I leave here. Sergeant, come over here. I want you to drive Mrs. Coppenger home."

"Sure, lieutenant, it will be my pleasure."

* * *

The coroner had talked to the paramedics and told them they were free to leave. His assistants brought out a black body bag; they placed Mary's body in it and zipped it up. Ron had been watching and was very thankful that Maggie had left and didn't have to witness this. It was bad enough finding her best friend like she did.

"One of you guys go down and bring that hostess, Ann, up here so I can talk to her. Round up all the hotel staff," Ron said. "Bring them in here to this ballroom and let's get statements from them. Maybe someone can get me some coffee."

* * *

Sergeant David Jamison escorted Maggie to a squad car that was parked in front of the hotel. Several men, dressed in business suits, stopped to watch as the red-eyed lady with the strange-looking red hat was helped into the police car. Maggie didn't notice them and Jamison was intent on the task ahead. After he had Maggie secure in the front seat he began the drive to deliver her home. Ron Waters had given him Maggie's address, so he used the squad car's navigation system to drive her home. Maggie was silent and the sergeant didn't press her for conversation. As they drove past Mary's house her eyes flooded with tears.

"Stop, please stop," Maggie begged. "This is where Mary lived, there in that yellow house. She's my best friend, we were like sisters. I can't believe she's dead. Sergeant Jamison, promise me, please, promise me that whoever killed her will be found and brought to justice!"

"I'm sorry about your friend. There's just no knowing what's in a murderer's mind. But I know Lieutenant Waters's reputation and he'll find them out, you can count on it. Now I'd better get you home," the sergeant said as he put the car in gear and continued on to Maggie's house.

Frank saw the squad car pull up in front of the house. He opened the door and went out onto the front porch. He saw Maggie in the front seat of the car and the policeman walking around to help her out. Frank ran down to meet them.

"Maggie," Frank yelled. "What's the matter?"

Maggie stepped out of the car and ran to her husband. "Oh Frank, I'm so glad you're home. It's awful. Mary's dead!"

Frank held her tight to him. He looked to the policeman who came to stand beside them. "What happened? Were they in an accident? Maggie, are you hurt?" His emotions suddenly spiked, he couldn't bear to see Maggie in such agony. This woman he loved, his other half, his heart. For over forty years he had loved this woman. Life without her would be unbearable. Mary was dead, and Frank wondered how it had happened. Had Maggie been in danger? No, Maggie was here, Maggie was safe. He held her tight, willing everything to be all right, willing all the pain and hurt to be gone.

"Like she said, Mr. Coppenger, her friend is dead, an apparent homicide. Lieutenant Ron Waters, he's your neighbor I understand, anyway he asked me to drive your wife home. She found the victim and is pretty upset; the lieutenant didn't think it advisable to allow her to drive herself home. The lieutenant will deliver your car to you himself."

"Thanks for bringing her home," Frank said as he shook the officer's hand. "You said Ron will bring our car to us later? I guess he will fill me in on what happened. I'd best get Maggie in the house so she can calm down and rest. Thanks again."

* * *

In the living room, Maggie sat down on the sofa but was still holding on to her husband for support. "Something horrible happened. I don't know what or how, but Mary is dead. I found her, she was just sitting there. I told her I was ready to leave. She didn't respond so I touched her arm. You know how she daydreams. There was blood all over her, all over that beautiful new outfit. It was the first time she wore it. She was dead, Frank!" Maggie shook and screamed, pounding on Frank's chest. "She was dead, Frank! Dead! One minute she was fine and the next she was dead!"

"Maggie, get hold of yourself, you need to change your clothes and wash up. Do you want to take a shower? You have blood all over you."

"She's dead, Frank! I said she's dead! Ron was there, he's a homicide detective. Ron wouldn't have come if they didn't think someone killed her. Someone killed her, murdered her!"

"Maggie, you have to calm down." Frank pulled her close to him, trying to quiet her. "If you don't get hold of yourself, I'll have to call the doctor."

"A bath, I want to take a bath. Let me sit in a tub of warm water. I'll feel better after a nice warm bath. Frank, there was this awful policeman there before Ron came and he acted like I killed her. It was just awful. I know he wanted to arrest me and he would have if Ron hadn't come when he did. I have to call Jessica and Susan. They left early, they don't know that Mary's dead. I have to tell them, Frank, I have to tell them!"

Frank feared Maggie was on the verge of a breakdown. He needed to get her to calm down. "Come on, baby, let's get you out of these clothes. I'll run you a nice warm bath." Frank helped his wife out of her clothes while the tub filled with warm water. He added her favorite scented bath salts, then he helped her into the tub. Frank sat on the side of the tub, carefully washing the blood off of Maggie's hands and arms.

* * *

The phone rang. Frank picked up the receiver. "Hello?"

"Frank, it's Rita. Is Maggie all right?"

"She's pretty shaken, Rita. She needs a little time to calm down," Frank told her.

Maggie stood beside Frank. "Let me talk to Rita, I need to tell her what happened."

Frank handed Maggie the phone. "Rita knows," he told her.

"Rita, do you know about Mary?" Maggie said into the phone.

"Yes, Maggie, are you all right? I just found out what happened. I was tied up with one of the waiters trying to gather up things that were left on the tables. Then I couldn't find my pantyhose doll. Someone moved her to the ladies room. I ran into Ron Waters, and he told me that Mary was dead. He asked me a lot of questions. He wants a list of everyone at the gathering. He said he has to question everyone. I think we are all suspects. I can't believe anyone would kill sweet Mary, that's just awful."

Maggie burst into tears again. Between sobs she said, "Rita, you have to come over right now! I have to call Jessica and Susan. I don't think they know yet. I need you to be here when I tell them." Maggie hung up the phone and asked Frank to call Jessica and Susan. He told them he couldn't explain over the phone but it was important that they come right over.

* * *

The three friends arrived at the same time. Frank answered the door and invited them to come inside. Maggie jumped up from where she was sitting and ran to her friends and hugged them tightly; her eyes were still red and swollen.

"Susan, oh Susan," Maggie said as she hugged her friend. "Jessica, I'm so glad to see you. Rita, are you all right?" Maggie moved from one friend to the other, hugging each one. "It's like a bad dream, a nightmare!"

"I know what you mean," Rita told her. "I've had a hard time keeping my emotions under control. When Ron told me Mary had been murdered I could hardly breath, it was such a shock."

"Murdered? What are you talking about, Rita? Maggie? What's going on?" Jessica asked.

"Frank, you didn't explain anything on the phone. Rita,

do you know what's going on? Where's Mary? What happened? You'd better tell us right now!" Susan demanded.

"I'm sorry, yes, Mary is dead," Frank stammered. "Maggie found Mary. Ron Waters came and said it looked like Mary had been murdered. Maggie was so upset Ron had one of the police officers drive her home. That's just about all I know."

"We just saw Mary this morning," Jessica said. "She was fine and having a great time."

"That party crasher I told you to look out for," Rita interrupted. "I'll bet she had something to do with it. She looked mighty suspicious to me. I tried to catch up with her but she vanished and no one seemed to know anything about her." Rita stood with her feet apart and her hands planted firmly on her hips.

Susan and Jessica both seemed to be in a daze. Susan sat down on the sofa and cried. "This is a nightmare, it can't be real! She was fine. She was with us having a great time. We were at the Sommerset Hotel, for God's sake! How can anyone get murdered at the Sommerset Hotel?"

Jessica was crying. Maggie gave her a tissue from the box she had been using. Rita sat down next to her. She put her arm around Jessica's shoulder and tried to comfort her, while Susan took her hand and began to rub it.

"Yes, it is unbelievable," Maggie said, "but it is true, I saw her. She was dead all right and I need to know who killed her! I need to clear my name."

"What do you mean, clear your name?" Rita asked.

"Well, girls, just for your information and please don't let it go any further, the police seem to think I'm the one that murdered Mary." Maggie's voice quivered and tears flooded her eyes.

"Oh my god," Susan said. "That's ridiculous! How could anyone think you could murder Mary? Mary's your best friend."

"I was there when the police came and I had Mary's blood on my hands. I'd appreciate it if you would all keep this to yourself and I really don't want to talk about it."

Finally, Jessica said. "We really must let Mary's family know. Maggie, you knew her so well—do you know anything about her family?"

Frank was feeling helpless with four crying women on his hands. "Come into the kitchen, girls. Help yourself to some coffee, it's fresh." Frank put four cups on the table along with cream and sugar.

"Thanks, Frank, you're a jewel," Jessica said as she reached for the cream. "A good cup of coffee is always soothing."

Maggie was feeling better now that her best friends were here and she had them to share this with. "Mary has brothers and a sister; both her parents passed away some time ago. There is a stepdaughter, Darlene. I'm not sure she will care much. We ran into her and her mother at the hotel. Mary said hello to them but they just brushed her off. Mary tried so hard to be friends with them but they never returned any kindness. I can get in touch with Mary's brother Paul. She gave me his phone number in case of an emergency. I guess this qualifies." The four friends sat talking and drinking coffee for a long time.

The doorbell rang and Frank went to answer it. "Ron, come in. Got any ideas about what happened?"

"Yeah, somebody killed her," Ron said. "I'm waiting to hear from the coroner for the exact cause of death but she was murdered, no question about that."

Maggie, feeling exhausted and drained of all her energy, asked, "Did you find any clues and what have they done with Mary's body? I just can't stand the thought of her in some cold, awful place."

"The lab guys dusted for fingerprints and went over everything with a fine-tooth comb. If there's a clue they will find it. We interviewed all the staff. Can any of you think of anything that might help? Rita, I need those names as soon as you can get them to me. Someone might have seen something."

"I still think it's that mystery woman. There was a strange woman there acting very weird. Nobody knew anything about her," Rita said.

"That's why I need those names," Ron explained. "The sooner we talk to people the sooner we find the person who did it."

"I'll get the list of names for you," Rita said.

"What about Mary's body?" Maggie asked again.

"The medical examiner has Mary's body," Ron told them. "He will have to determine the exact cause of death."

"So does that mean they will do an autopsy?" Maggie asked.

"Yes, they will have to do an autopsy," Ron said.

The women all looked at each other, not wanting to talk about what they thought that meant. They had all watched enough CSI shows on television and read enough mysteries to have a good idea.

"Has anyone notified Mary's family?" Jessica asked.

"No, I don't think so. Maggie, I thought you would know who to contact and it would be easier on her family if you would take care of it rather than having the police knock on their door."

"We were just talking about that. I know Mary's brother Paul. I spent a lot of my childhood out at the farm where he lives." Maggie looked at Frank. "Frank and I can drive out to the farm and tell them in person. I'm not looking forward to it, but you're right; it would be awful to have a stranger tell them. That would be too cruel."

"Sure, Ron, we will drive out there and tell Mary's family," Frank assured him. "Thanks for bringing the car back, and I really appreciate you taking care of Maggie like you did."

Ron eased his way toward the front door. In a hushed

voice he told Frank, "You know, Maggie is the prime suspect. The only reason she wasn't arrested is because I know her personally and could vouch for her. I know she could never, under any circumstances, commit murder."

"In that case, Ron, you'd better get out there and find out who did."

Chapter 4

Maggie dreaded telling Paul about Mary, but she knew she had to do it and there was no putting it off. With renewed determination she looked at Frank—somehow she drew strength from him—and she knew together they would get through this. This man, her husband, he would be beside her, holding her, loving her. Together with God's help they would both get through this.

"Frank, I don't want to call Paul to tell him we're coming, he will know something's wrong. We'd best drive out to the farm and hope he's home."

"Good idea. Do you remember how to get there? I haven't seen Paul in a long time. He's a great guy; I'd like to have a good visit with him under different circumstances."

"I haven't been out there for a long time, but I made many trips there when we were kids. I think I could still find it with my eyes closed."

The drive to the farm only took about twenty minutes. Maggie could see the big white farmhouse sitting in the midst of the rolling wheat fields. Big shade trees surrounded the house and a lush green lawn out front made the place feel like home to Maggie. The front porch extended the entire length of the house. Baskets overflowing with flowers hung from the eaves. A swing and two wicker chairs with a wicker table between them made the front porch an inviting place to relax in the evening after dinner.

A lump formed in Maggie's throat as she remembered sitting on the swing with Mary. They were just kids. Their feet didn't touch the porch floor. They would lean forward and then push back, making the swing go back and forth. They would laugh and laugh like girls do. One of them would jump off the swing and push hard, then climb back on hoping to get it going higher. As teenagers they would swing and whisper secrets about the cute boys at school. Giggling and whispering their plans about what to wear, they loved to dress alike, like sisters.

"Oh, Frank, I have so many happy memories of this place. I spent many summers out here with Mary. The Andersons weren't well off but I'll tell you growing up in the country has its rewards. See that big tree in the front of the house? I think I still have scars on my legs and arms from climbing it. Mary and I would spend hours up there until Paul and his buddies would climb up. Of course we wouldn't think of sharing a tree house with boys."

"Those boys probably didn't want to share it with you girls, either."

"You're right, but even as a kid Paul was a gentleman. Mary and I were several years older so we didn't have much in common with him. I have good memories of all the Anderson kids."

"I never met the others. Isn't there another brother and a sister?" Frank asked.

"Yes, they're both married and moved away. Mary kept in touch but she was always much closer to Paul, probably because he stayed on the farm. Paul's wife, Ellie, and Mary were like sisters.

"Ellie's family still lives on a neighboring farm. It was Ellie's brothers that were always hanging around with Paul. Ellie and her brothers were in 4-H. They had all kinds of animals, everything from rabbits to a prize bull. Ellie was very serious about her responsibility to her 4-H projects. At least once a week I'd ride the bus home with Mary. Ellie would stay on the bus and go home to tend to her chores. Sometimes her brothers would get off the bus with Paul. Ellie would finish her chores and ride her bike back to play with Mary and me. Ellie is such a fine lady now, so dependable and faithful."

As they pulled up in front of the house, they saw Paul coming from the barn. Ellie came out of the house, drying her hands on a kitchen towel. Both of them were wondering who had just pulled into their driveway. Paul recognized them and came around to the driver's side of the car to greet Frank.

"Frank, are you lost? It's sure good to see you, been a long time. Maggie, seems like old times, you out here at the farm."

Ellie greeted Maggie. "It's so good to see you, Maggie, come inside. I've got some nice cold lemonade. We can have a good talk."

Paul said, "I need a break from the heat of the barn and would love a cool drink."

Ellie led the way, chatting about how happy she was to see them. "We don't get many visitors. Becky's friends are all in town and they don't come out much anymore. Now that she's working at that little boutique, she's hardly here. Just listen to me carry on. Come in, come in. It's been too long. Have a seat, I'll just pour the lemonade and we can do some catching up."

Paul stomped on the mat outside the door and wiped his boots before entering the kitchen. He hung his soiled cowboy hat on a hook by the door.

"Let me wash my hands and I'll join you. Frank, how's that pretty red convertible coming? You 'bout got it finished?"

"Just got it back from the painter, guy did a real good job."

"Bet that cost a pretty penny," Paul said.

"I did all the prep work so that saved a lot. Next time you're in town why don't you stop by? We'll take her out for a little spin."

"Sounds good."

Ellie began pouring iced lemonade into tall glasses.

"This really hits the spot, Ellie," Frank said.

Sitting at the large kitchen table, Maggie suddenly felt homesick. "I love it here. Your kitchen is so comfortable and cozy." Maggie rubbed her hand over the wooden tabletop. Paul's grandfather had made the table many years ago to accommodate a growing family. Paul had refinished it; the grain of the wood ran smooth. Originally, there had been benches on either side of the table and a large armchair at each end. Those had been replaced by six carved wooden chairs that Ellie had put cushions on. Matching curtains were pulled back to the sides of the window that was over the kitchen sink. Upgraded appliances and new tile flooring added a bit of elegance to the room.

Tears flooded Maggie's eyes. She was having a hard time controlling her emotions and she hadn't even begun to tell them about Mary. How could she do this, where would she start?

"Maggie, it's been a long time, how are you? It's so good to see you. What can we do for you?" Paul looked and sounded just like she remembered: a strong, happy, hard-working, good-natured guy.

"Paul, I've got bad news. It's Mary. I don't know how to tell you, where to start."

"Just tell me, don't hold back." Paul's voice was demanding yet gentle. "Has Mary had an accident, a stroke? Go ahead and tell me. Where is she?"

"Paul, Mary's dead." Maggie couldn't hold it back any longer—tears flooded her eyes and she began to cry. "She's been murdered, Paul. Someone killed her. She's dead. The police took her body and they are questioning everyone. I found her. She was just sitting there. There were roses in a big bowl on a table. You know how she is about roses." Maggie looked at Ellie, who nodded in agreement. "I thought she was sitting there admiring the roses. I sat down and started talking to her. I said, 'I'm ready to leave, Mary.' She didn't say anything and when I touched her she was cold. There was blood all over her beautiful new blouse."

"Wait a minute," Paul interrupted. "Where were you? Where did this happen?"

"We were at the Sommerset Hotel for brunch with the Red Hats. We were having a great time. There were about two hundred women there. Most everyone had left. Oh Paul, I'm so sorry." Maggie rubbed both eyes with her hands and took a deep breath. "Paul, Ellie, I'm sorry. I'm so sorry."

Maggie felt she was rambling. She wanted to get it all said. She wanted Paul and Ellie to know all the details. Was it too much for them to understand? Good, decent people like Paul and Ellie couldn't understand murder. Maggie couldn't understand it, but she saw it, she felt it. It still weighed heavy on her, that dark evil presence that surrounded Mary. It lingered even after her death. It wanted to drag Maggie down into the depth of the place where its hate could fester in her heart and mind. Maggie didn't realize it but there was a struggle going on deep within her, a struggle between good and evil, a struggle of emotions. Would anger, hate, and revenge take over or would love and forgiveness prevail?

Frank knew the inner struggle that was going on in his wife's mind. He squeezed her hand to reassure her. Together they would get through this.

"We didn't want them to send some stranger out to tell you," Frank said. "Ron Waters is in charge of the investigation. He said it will be a few days before they will release Mary's body."

Paul stared down at his hands. He couldn't believe what he was hearing. "Murdered? Who in the world would murder Mary? That's ridiculous. Mary didn't have any enemies. Darlene was the only person I can think of who didn't like Mary, but murder? I think Darlene is just a spoiled kid. I don't think she would resort to murder. That person, Edith with the dog that dug up Mary's roses, but that was quite a while back. I sure can't think of anyone mean enough to murder her. You said Ron Waters is in charge of the investigation. Was he there? Did you talk to him?"

Ellie put her hand over her mouth to hold back the scream that wanted to escape. Tears were rolling down her cheeks but she didn't make a sound. She used the towel to wipe the tears from her face.

"Yes, I talked to Ron," Maggie said. "There was blood all over Mary's blouse. They said she had been stabbed with something. I don't know, Paul, it was all a nightmare. You will want to talk to Ron, maybe you should call him."

"Yes, I'll call him. I'll have to call the rest of the family. I can't believe it. Mary murdered." Paul was crying. Ellie took his hand and squeezed.

"We'll go now," Frank said. "We didn't want some stranger to come and tell you. You've got a lot to do. I'm so sorry. If there is anything we can do, you make sure you call us," Frank said as he shook Paul's hand. Maggie and Ellie hugged each other, blending their tears as their faces touched.

Frank and Maggie drove down the long driveway with only the crunch of gravel to break the silence. "I didn't tell them," Maggie said as they turned onto the paved road.

"You didn't tell them what?"

"I didn't tell them the police suspect me of killing Mary. I just couldn't tell them that. What would they think of me if I told them I am the prime suspect?"

"There was no need to tell them. Because it's ridiculous! Even Ron said he didn't believe you killed her."

"I'm just so ashamed that anyone would think I could commit murder."

"It's only the ones that don't know you, sweetheart, and it's their job to suspect everyone."

"We have to find out who did it, Frank. Otherwise this

will hang over my head and they might even convict me on circumstantial evidence."

Chapter 5

Paul was in shock. He was too stunned to ask all the questions he was thinking of now. He wondered what really happened. *Someone killed Mary? That's crazy, why would anyone kill Mary?* he wondered.

"I need to know what happened. I have to talk to Ron Waters. I don't know Ron, but Mary had talked about him on several occasions and he sounds like a pretty decent guy. Ron lives next door to Frank and Maggie. I could call them to get his number or maybe I should go to the police station. Right now we have to tell Becky. After I have more information, I'll call the rest of the family. It will take them a day or two to get here and I know they will all want to come," Paul told Ellie.

* * *

Paul and Ellie had been high school sweethearts. In fact they were sweethearts long before high school, but that was when it became evident to everyone that knew them.

There was never any question between them. Ellie never looked at another boy and Paul never looked at another girl. They were good together. The life of a small farmer was a hard life, but they stuck together. It seemed like the harder life was, the closer they grew.

"I need to see for myself," Paul said. "I need to talk to Ron Waters. I want to see Mary."

He looked up the number for the police department and dialed it. When the call went through he asked to speak to Ron Waters.

"Homicide, Waters, can I help you?"

"Is this Ron Waters?"

"Yes, who is this?"

"This is Paul Anderson. Maggie Coppenger just told me about my sister, Mary Reed. I can't believe…"

"Yes, Paul, I asked Maggie to contact you. We thought that would be easier on you than sending someone out from the station. It was pretty rough on Maggie. She found Mary. You know they were pretty close."

"You're telling me that Mary was murdered? What happened? Mary didn't have any enemies. I want to see her, where is she?" Paul demanded.

"Sure, come on down, she's at the county morgue. Maggie made a positive ID at the scene, so we're sure it's Mary. I'll let the ME know you're coming. Then if you could stop by my office I'd appreciate it."

Paul hung up the phone and stood there for a long minute. As he turned to face Ellie tears ran down both his cheeks. Ellie put her arms around his waist and buried her face in his chest. They held tight to each other hoping somehow to ease the pain of a loss they couldn't fully comprehend.

"What did Ron say?" Ellie asked.

"He said Maggie identified her and they are positive it's Mary. I'm going down to the coroner's to see for myself," Paul said as he wiped his tears with his shirtsleeve.

Ellie handed him a box of tissues she had retrieved from the cupboard. "I'll go with you," she said as she started removing the apron she was wearing.

"No, I don't want you to see her like that. She's my sister. She took care of me when I was little, when Mom was too sick. I've just got to go and see what they did to her. You need to stay here in case Becky comes home."

"Becky, oh my goodness, Becky will be devastated. She and Mary were so close." Ellie ran her fingers through her short brown hair. "This is a nightmare, Paul. I just can't believe it."

Paul was a big man, six feet five inches tall, with a firm, muscular build from years of physical farm labor. His blond hair, blue eyes, and strong, wide-set jaw identified his Norwegian ancestry. He could hold his own with anyone. But right now he was feeling helpless and vulnerable.

"Mary was like a sister to me, too. You know how I loved her."

"I know, Ellie, but this is something I have to do by myself. It won't be pleasant. I don't want you to have to see her this way and I don't want you to go to the police station. It will be hard enough seeing her at the funeral home. I'll have to hurry to catch Ron before he leaves."

"Okay, I'll be here when you get back. I love you."

Paul gave Ellie a kiss on her cheek, then took the keys to his pickup off a hook by the kitchen door. He paused a moment before going out to his truck to head for town.

As Ellie watched Paul drive away she was left with a hollow feeling in the pit of her stomach. Loneliness and fear swept over her. Suddenly she was frightened of being alone. She tried hard to convince herself she was safe. As the old farmhouse creaked, she strained her ears for unfamiliar sounds. Suddenly a flock of birds fluttered and squawked; the dog barked. A rustling of tree branches scraped against the side of the house. Ellie shivered, her eyes darting back and forth from one window to another.

This is silly, she thought. *I've lived in the country all my life. We've never had any cause for worry. No one has ever threatened us. We've never been in any danger here.* "But someone murdered Mary," Ellie said aloud. She walked into the living room and checked to make sure the front door was locked, then she went back to the kitchen to check the door there. *All secure,* she thought. *I have to be strong for Paul and Becky.*

The phone rang and Ellie wondered who it might be. What would she say about Mary? Would she have to tell a neighbor or a family member that Mary had been murdered? She waited for the phone to ring three times before she picked it up. When she put the receiver to her ear she heard a click and then the dial tone. Ellie replaced the receiver. Fear shook her and she began to cry. Great sobs came from deep inside her. She was feeling the loss of her sister-in-law, Mary, a friend from childhood, a friend long before she became a relative. The sister she never had. Ellie couldn't grasp the idea of murder—it was so foreign to her—and she couldn't stand the idea of being alone any longer. She went to the door that led from the kitchen to the back yard. Her faithful dog, Sam, was lying near the step. Sam was Ellie's dog, a big German Shepherd mix. Someone had dumped him, half starved, at their driveway when he was just a pup. Ellie had brought him into her warm kitchen, gave him food and water. She found an old quilt and made a bed in the corner. Sam had been her faithful companion ever since.

"Sam, come in here, I need some company. I've got the jitters. You remember Mary, don't you? Well, someone killed her. I hope the rest of us aren't in any danger, and I'll feel better with you right here beside me." The dog got up slowly, stretched, then bounded up the steps into the kitchen.

Ellie gave Sam a loving pat on the head and scratched behind his ear. She reached for the box of dog biscuits, took one out, and handed it to Sam. He took it in his mouth but dropped it to the floor, then nuzzled his nose against Ellie's leg and made a whining sound. "Oh Sam, you know how I feel, don't you?" She kept talking to the dog and he was alert to her every move. The wind picked up and blew a stray piece of paper across the windowpane, creating a shadow that startled her. The hair on the back of Sam's neck stood up, and a growl escaped his throat. He moved in front of Ellie, ready to take on any intruder.

Ellie sat down on one of the kitchen chairs. Her heart was broken and her emotions were raw. Sam, sensing there was no trouble coming from outside, turned and laid his head on Ellie's lap. She scratched the dog behind his ears again and spoke softly to him and then she picked up the biscuit from the floor and gave it to Sam, indicating for him to lie on his bed in the corner. Ellie felt better with Sam in the house. When he finished his biscuit he stayed on his bed with his chin on his front paws, watching every move she made. She continued talking to the dog while she started fixing supper. She didn't know how long Paul would be in town but she hoped he would feel like eating something when he came home, and she needed something to do to keep herself busy.

There was always plenty of food around the Anderson house. Every year Paul butchered a beef and a small pig to make bacon and ham. Ellie raised chickens so there were eggs and chickens for frying. She wasn't squeamish about using an axe on a chicken's neck. Her garden provided fresh vegetables all summer, and shelves in the basement held jars full of green beans, corn, carrots, beets, and pickles. They were always ready to share their bounty with anyone in need. Ellie wasn't a gourmet cook, but no one ever complained when they sat down to eat at her table.

The crunch of tires on the gravel driveway caused Sam's ears to perk up. Ellie stopped what she was doing and looked out the window that faced the large green lawn and driveway. Sam rose and faced the door, on guard. The hair on his neck stood up.

He felt the tension in the air caused by Ellie's nervous behavior. After a few minutes they heard a car door slam and the sound of footsteps in gravel coming toward the house. Sam moved in front of Ellie; he knew he was her protector. Ellie held her breath as she watched the doorknob turn, then someone pushed hard against the door. Sam growled as the knob turned again.

"Who's there?" Ellie cried. "Who's there?"

The sound of footsteps walking away through the gravel made Ellie breath a sigh of relief. A car door slammed. She looked out the window but couldn't see where the car was parked. She waited for the sound of the car's motor to start but the sound of footsteps walking in gravel again made Ellie's stomach turn. She took hold of Sam's collar to steady herself when a key inserted into the lock made a jiggling sound, but the extra deadbolt held the door shut.

"Who's there?" Ellie screamed.

"Mom, it's me. Why is the door locked? Let me in."

"Becky, it's Becky. It's okay, Sam, Becky's home."

Sam relaxed and wagged his tail. The tone in Ellie's voice, now relaxed and happy, let the dog know his mistress was feeling better.

Becky came through the kitchen door and immediately noticed her mother's swollen eyes.

"Mom, what's going on? You've been crying." Sam came alongside Becky and leaned into her leg. She began to stroke the dog's back. "What's going on, Sam? Who made Mom cry?"

Ellie put her arms around Becky and gave her a hug. Holding her daughter tight, she said, "Becky, it's bad, real bad."

"Where's Dad?" Becky yelled, pushing her mother away. "What's happened? Where's Dad?"

"Dad's okay, he's gone to town. It's your Aunt Mary. She's dead, Becky, she's dead."

"Dead? I just saw her yesterday. She was fine. She was going to some big deal with her Red Hat group. She wanted me to go with her. Maggie was supposed to pick her up. Were they in a car wreck?"

"No, it wasn't like that." Ellie sat down hard on a chair. "Someone killed her."

"Mom, what do you mean? Someone killed her, like an accident?"

"Becky, I don't know! Your dad has gone to talk to the

police and to the coroner to see for himself. I wanted to go with him but he wouldn't let me."

"How did you find out? Who told you?"

"Maggie and Frank came out. They didn't want some strange policeman to tell us. They thought it would be better if they came out."

"Maggie? Wasn't Aunt Mary with Maggie? Where did it happen, when?"

"Yes, Maggie found her. They were at the Sommerset Hotel. Maggie found Mary sitting in a chair all bloody. When the police came they said she was dead."

"I should have gone with her. She asked me to go with her. She bought me a new hat and sweater. She wanted me to go and I made some lame excuse. It's my fault. If I had been there I could have done something. Oh, Mom, I'm so sorry. What will we do without Aunt Mary?"

Ellie put her arms around her daughter and they clung to each other. "Becky, it's not your fault."

"Aunt Mary was always doing nice things for me. She spent a lot of money on me and I never appreciated it. Now she's dead and she'll never know that I really loved her."

"Oh, Becky, she knew that you loved her." Sam whimpered and nuzzled his face against Ellie's leg. "Yes, Sam, we know you loved Mary, too."

* * *

Mary's family had arrived and most of them were staying at the farm. Mary's body was finally released and funeral arrangements were being made. Maggie and Ellie met at Mary's house. Maggie opened the front door and they both walked in. The house had always been warm and cheery when Mary was alive. Now in her absence it was cold and dark.

"I always loved to visit Mary here. When she recovered from Hank's death she really cheered up and had a renewed zest for life," Maggie told Ellie.

"I didn't have many chances to come here. We're always so busy at the farm. Mary would come out for a Sunday dinner and a visit at least once a month. She and Paul were so close. I don't think a week went by that Becky didn't stop in to visit her," Ellie said.

"Mary loved that girl like she was her own," Maggie assured her.

"Yes, Mary was like a second mother to Becky. We had better find a dress. The funeral home wants it by this afternoon."

As they stepped into Mary's bedroom, Maggie felt like they were invading the private world Mary had shared with her late husband Hank. Their wedding pictures still hung on the wall over a small roll-top desk that was a gift from Mary to Hank on a wedding anniversary. A quilt made in the wedding ring pattern by Mary's mother was on the bed. A heart-shaped pillow embroidered with their names and the date of their wedding was on the bed where Mary had placed it. Ellie walked to the closet and slowly opened the door. She touched several items that hung there. Ellie took a dress from the closet and removed the protective plastic covering. She held the dress up on its hanger for Maggie to see.

"Maggie, I love this dress. Mary wore it to Paul's and my twenty-fifth anniversary party. She just looked beautiful in it."

"I remember when she bought it. She was excited about the party and all the surprises Becky had planned for you."

Tears came to Ellie's eyes as she remembered that day. "That was such a happy time. Mary was such a sweet, gentle person. I can't imagine why anyone would murder her."

"I can't either, and I pray that whoever did it will be found out."

Maggie and Ellie tried their best to comfort each other. Each woman knew the other had a very special relationship with Mary.

"You know Mary left everything to Becky," Maggie said.

"Yes, Mary told us some time ago," Ellie said. "Becky's awfully young to have so much responsibility—the house and Mary's investments."

"You and Paul have good heads on your shoulders. I'm sure you'll keep her grounded."

"We're trying to sort it all out. She'd love to move into an apartment; the house and all its responsibilities are a little overwhelming at Becky's age. Then there's all the furniture and Mary's personal things. There are a lot of decisions to be made. I'm glad Mary made you her executor. Becky has a lot of respect for you." Ellie was still holding the dress.

"I think this is the dress, Ellie. It will remind us all of a happier time." Maggie closed the closet door, making the decision final.

On the drive to the funeral home both women were silent, thoughts of Mary racing through their minds.

Mary's funeral was a celebration of a beautiful life. The minister asked for anyone that would like to say a word about her. The church was full of her students and fellow teachers. One after another they stood to tell of her impact on their lives. Many of her students, now grown, told of her encouragement over the years. Mary was the kind of teacher that kept in touch with her students, encouraging them, cheering them on.

She attended their graduations and their weddings. She knew the names of their spouses and children. When they left her classroom they didn't leave her life. Mary never had a child of her own but she had hundreds of students that she cherished as her own.

Everyone in attendance seemed to swell in pride at being a part of her life, a life cut short, but a life that had such a positive influence on so many.

Chapter 6

Once each year there is a rodeo in Sommer, Washington. The parade on Saturday morning starts off the festivities. Cowboys and cowgirls come from miles around, pulling big horse trailers behind their pickup trucks. Rodeo queens from big and small towns all over the state come decked out in their brightly colored hats with sparkles embroidered on their shirts. Each queen has a sash hanging over her shoulder and across her breast naming the town she hails from. Of course, Miss Sommer Rodeo and Miss Washington Rodeo always get the loudest cheers. Horses prance down the street with their braided tails and manes. Some have sparkling hearts and stars painted on their rumps. The mayor and representatives from the city and county ride in convertibles and vintage cars; the police and fire departments come out in full force.

The Red Hats found their spot in the parade right behind the Cub Scouts who would be riding on a wagon pulled by a John Deere tractor.

Rita had arranged for an old-fashioned trolley car for those Red Hats who were unable to walk the parade route. The Mystery Mamas would be riding in Frank's red Mustang convertible. Some of the other Red Hat groups rode in convertibles and of course there were those who would walk and carry banners with their chapter's name on them, some twirling parasols and boas while passing out candy to spectators and tooting their kazoos.

"I'm so glad we planned this a long time ago, my heart just isn't in it without Mary," Maggie said.

Jessica took a head count of the Red Hats. They were all

wearing bright purple western shirts and red cowgirl hats. "I know Mary's here in spirit. She loved this sort of thing," Jessica said, holding the car door open for the others to climb in the back seat. Susan and Lisa sat in the back of the open convertible with Rita sitting on the back of the seat with her feet between her two friends. They had big bags of candy that they would throw to the crowd standing along the parade route.

Frank had agreed to let Maggie drive his bright red 1966 Mustang GT convertible in the parade. Frank had been a Mustang lover since the first model came out. He had several of the classic cars but this one was his pride and joy. The white interior, bucket seats, and fancy wheels made it look like something a movie star would drive. He had let Maggie drive it once when he finished restoring it but he was at her side watching every move. This was his baby, the only one that turned out just the way he wanted. When Maggie had asked him if she could drive it in the parade he wasn't thrilled about the prospect.

"Frank, I'll just drive down to Main Street and get in the line. You know the parade only moves five miles an hour and I'll be very careful. The girls know how particular you are about your car. I'll drop them off and come right back home after the parade."

"All right, I just don't want kids putting their hands all over it and scratching the paint. That paint job cost a fortune," Frank said as he used his chamois to do a little more shining before she drove off.

The parade was great fun and Maggie tried hard to get into the spirit of things. She waved to the crowd with the fringe on her shirtsleeve blowing in the wind. Some of the people in the crowd yelled and whistled. Children lined the sides of the street, waiting for candy to be thrown to them. Everyone was in a festive mood. Clowns were running around shaking hands with the younger children. The firemen and police were sounding their sirens. Smokey Bear and the dalmatian dog were riding on one of the fire trucks. There were vendors with little booths set up selling cotton candy, soft drinks, snow cones, hot dogs, and lots of other things to tempt the parade watchers. There were other booths selling handmade crafts and the library was selling its excess books. Clowns were making balloon animals and others were doing face painting. All in all it looked like a good day in Sommer.

"Maggie, please thank Frank for letting us ride in his Mustang. It is really an eye catcher. It must have been hard for him to let you take it," Rita said.

"I'll tell him that we were a big hit and his car got lots of whistles."

"Oh come on, you know they were whistling at us. We always get whistles when we go out in our red hats," Rita said as she threw her last handful of candy to the crowd.

"Rita, you should know the most important thing to a man is his car. If it's a classic car, one that he's spent a small fortune on, not to mention the hundreds of hours laboring over every little detail."

"Please, don't ask him to choose between his car and his firstborn," Susan joked.

"Okay, okay, I hear what you're saying, the car got the whistles, thank Frank for us. I enjoyed this ride much better than last year's."

"Don't remind me, last year we rode on a hay wagon—of course a Mustang convertible is much nicer," Jessica added. "I never want to ride on another hay wagon as long as I live. I itched for days after that ride!"

"Rita, I know those gals appreciated you arranging for the trolley. That is so neat the way the step came down so Helen could get on with her wheelchair," Susan said.

"We don't ever want to leave anyone out of the fun because of their physical limitations," Rita said. "That's not the Red Hat way."

"Hear, hear," they all said in unison, then gave a few toots on their kazoos.

After the parade Maggie drove the girls to Rita's car. "Why don't we have some lunch at Zips? French fries, tartar sauce, and a big juicy burger?" Jessica suggested.

"They have a terrific BLT," Lisa said.

"Sounds good to me," Rita agreed. "I'm starving; those few pieces of candy didn't last long."

"You were eating the candy?" Susan asked. "No wonder we ran out before the end of the route."

"I only ate a few pieces. I was starving! Don't tell me you didn't eat any," Rita said accusingly.

"Okay, okay," Susan said. "Let's go get some lunch."

"I'm going to lunch at the Sommerset. I'm going to snoop around and ask some questions. It may amount to nothing but at least it's better than sitting around moping," Maggie said. "Maybe something will jog my memory. I've just got to know who killed Mary. Besides, I promised Frank I'd bring his car home as soon as the parade was over."

"You can't go down there by yourself, Maggie. I'm going with you. But let's go home and change clothes first," Jessica said as she got into the front seat of the Mustang. She waved to the others as they drove away.

"Let us know if you have any luck! We'll talk later," Lisa yelled as Maggie pulled away. Lisa was feeling a little left out of things, since she had been out of town when Mary was murdered. "I'm worried about Maggie. She is really hurting over Mary's death."

"Maggie and Mary were like sisters, and finding Mary like she did was such a shock. She really needs to get some grief counseling, but of course she won't go to a counselor. She said she talked to her pastor. He prayed with her and gave her some scripture and a book on grief. I'm worried about her, too," Susan said.

"I think Maggie will be all right when the murderer is found and brought to justice, and the sooner the better if you ask me," Rita said.

Maggie dropped Jessica off at her house and promised to be back in half an hour. She drove home and when she opened the garage door she was surprised to see that her SUV was gone. *Frank didn't say anything about going any place. He's probably gone for some lunch,* Maggie thought as she went into the house, where she found a note on the kitchen counter.

"Hope you had fun at the parade—gone to town, new Mustangs are out. F"

Maggie went to the bedroom. "Frank just can't stay away from the car shop. Well, if you're not back by the time I'm dressed I'm taking your little Mustang to town, Mr. F."

Maggie chose a nice little dress with a matching jacket, slipped it over her head, and applied more lipstick and hairspray. The jacket had a Red Hat pin on the lapel so she decided to go with the Red Hat earrings that matched. She slipped her feet into a pair of black sandals with a little heel and Velcro straps. It didn't seem to matter which shoes she wore, her feet would be hurting by the time she got back home. She would pick up Jessica and they would start asking questions.

* * *

Jessica Wyatt lived in a small cottage behind her daughter and son-in-law's home. Theirs was a large house on a half-acre lot so there was plenty of room for the little one-bedroom cottage that Jessica called home. It had a small kitchen and a dining area large enough for her table and the hutch that held all her lovely china. The living room where she watched television and read was warm and cozy. There was another room that she called her sewing room. She didn't do much sewing these days, but she could if she wanted. It was perfect for Jessica—she had her privacy, and she was close to Lori and Tom and her granddaughters. After her husband passed away she didn't want to live in their big house all alone. The cottage was perfect for her now and some day when she no longer needed it, Lori and Tom could rent it out.

Jessica Wyatt had been a widow for seven years. Her husband Steve, a dentist, had left Jessica financially well off. She had never worked outside the home. Her home and family had always been enough for her. Her granddaughters were the light of her life, but they were in high school and busy with all the things teenage girls do. Jessica didn't look like a grandmother. She wore her auburn hair in the same pageboy cut that she'd worn since her school days. It suited her. She had good skin tone and her figure was firm, thanks to her workout sessions at Curves. At sixty, Jessica was enjoying life. She had her family and a comfortable home. She was blessed with good friends. Her Red Hat club and the Mystery Readers book club took up most of her spare time. Jessica was full of energy; she was determined that old age wouldn't get her down. Her positive attitude was contagious and everyone that came in contact with her seemed to take on the same zest for life that she had.

Chapter 7

Frank hadn't come back with Maggie's SUV, so she picked up the phone and called Jessica. "Hi Jess, it's me. Are you ready?"

"I'm ready. I'll meet you out front."

Jessica was waiting when Maggie pulled up to the curb. "What on earth are you doing driving Frank's Mustang to town?" Jessica opened the door of the Mustang and lowered herself into the passenger seat. After she fastened her seatbelt she turned to Maggie and asked, "Where's your rig?"

"Frank wasn't home when I got there. He left a note saying he'd gone to look at the new Mustangs. So I left him a note saying I'm going to lunch."

"I don't feel good about this, Maggie, but it's between you and Frank."

On the drive to the Sommerset Hotel Maggie couldn't get the murder out of her mind. "Can you think of any reason someone would want to murder Mary? People don't just kill for no reason. If it was a drive-by shooting or a hit and run, I'd say okay, it was a mistake or an accident. But the way she was killed. No, whoever did it was right up close. This was no mistake. This was no accident."

"No, I can't imagine why anyone would kill Mary. It doesn't make sense. I've known Mary for a long time, not as long as you, but I can't imagine Mary having any enemies. Why, she taught my Lori when she was just a child."

"Mary never traveled and she never had company, except for close friends and family. Her whole life since she retired from teaching was her garden and the Red Hats, and of course her students were always a big part of her life."

"Maggie, do you think Mary could have been involved in something that we didn't know about?" Jessica spoke quietly as if someone might be listening. "After all, we didn't spend every minute with her."

"Do you mean something weird or illegal? No, there is no possibility of her being involved with something like that."

"Maybe she was growing marijuana around her roses for extra money. Maybe someone had something against her from her past, blackmail or something."

"Oh, Jess, don't be ridiculous. Marijuana in Mary's roses? Besides, Mary didn't have a past, so who could blackmail her anyway?"

"Everyone has a past, Maggie."

"What are you trying to say? You think Mary was into some sort of criminal activity? Or maybe she was a spy for the government and some spy from some other country came after her. Maybe the mafia put a contract out on her? Get real, Jess."

"Well, like you said, people just don't get murdered for no reason. Someone had it in for Mary!"

"That's the reason I wanted to come back here today. Maybe we can make some sense out of it. Maybe we need to think like a killer. Then maybe we can figure it out."

"Oh sure, think like a killer. Here we are, Maggie. I wish this place didn't hold such bad memories. It's so elegant and the food is always excellent. But I don't think any of us will be able to enjoy it again for a very long time."

Maggie pulled the Mustang into the parking garage. Before she could put it in park, a young man opened the door for her.

"Wow, lady, she's a beauty."

"No fingerprints and no scratches!" Maggie said while shaking a finger at the boy. "Or my husband will kill me first and then he will come looking for you."

"Gotcha, I understand. I'll guard her with my life." He

The Hat Pin Murders

gave Maggie a wink and carefully drove the Mustang to a remote parking spot.

Inside the lobby of the hotel they were greeted by the same young lady as the last time they were there, Ann. She was still wearing the burgundy suit and the nametag. "Good afternoon. Are you ladies here for lunch?"

Maggie decided the burgundy suit must be a uniform, because she noticed the doorman was wearing a burgundy jacket and trousers.

"Good afternoon. Yes, we had hoped to have lunch but we don't have reservations. We were here several weeks ago with our Red Hat group. It was our friend that was killed. I believe you were on duty that day, too. I was hoping to ask you a few questions."

"I told the police everything I know. I really didn't see anything that day. Someone said to call 911 and I ran to the office and called. That's all I know. I'm really sorry about your friend."

"But Ann, your post seems to be here in the front to greet people and give directions when they come in. When I found Mary's body you were up on the second floor. Why were you up there?" Maggie asked.

"Oh, yes, I remember you. You were the one that was there by that dead lady. It's kinda funny that you were there with blood all over you. Don't talk to me like you're so high and mighty. I think you killed her and you're trying to place the blame on someone else," Ann accused. Ann seemed upset with the questioning. "I was on my break. I went upstairs to look in on the Red Hat party," she retorted hotly. "The Red Hats always do skits and have some sort of entertainment. I just wanted to see what was going on."

"The party was over," Maggie interrupted, "and most of the Red Hats had left. If you had been there to see the entertainment and were still there when I found Mary's body, you might have seen something. I'm not accusing, I just want to know what really happened. You might have seen the murderer. And no, it wasn't me. I didn't kill her."

"I told the police everything I know. I'm sorry I can't be of more help but I really don't want to get involved. Now, if you would like to have lunch I'll escort you to the dining room."

Maggie and Jessica were seated in the dining room and ordered iced tea and salad. Jessica opened a packet of sweetener and poured it into her tea. As she stirred she watched the little white granules swirl around.

"Maggie, she knows more than she's telling. She seemed upset at your questions. I think she saw something. Maybe we need to talk to her again on our way out."

"Yes, I got the same feeling. She seemed nervous about my questions. I can't imagine why she would have still been up there when I found Mary's body. If she came up to watch the entertainment…." Maggie pondered the idea. "The party had been over quite a while and almost everyone had left by then. I think she's lying. She knows more than she's telling."

"And then maybe she just doesn't want to get involved. Some people are like that," Jessica said.

"Yes, but I think she's holding something back. Can't hurt to talk to her again." Maggie pushed her salad around on her plate.

"How's your salad? The last time I had a salad here I took half of it home. But I don't think I will this time. I'm starving. I think I'll be able to eat it all. Wasn't the parade fun? I'm always surprised at the floats different organizations put together. Our community is small but everyone comes together to make it a success."

Jessica was hoping to get Maggie to talk about something other than Mary's death so they could enjoy their lunch.

"Yes, it was a nice parade, but until I know who killed Mary I won't be able to really enjoy any of the things we did together. I'm sorry, Jess. I'm not very good company." Maggie took a bite of her salad without tasting it.

"I can't imagine the shock of finding Mary the way you did. But I'm afraid you're going to make yourself sick. You've become obsessed. It's all you talk about and you're not eating."

"It was the worst thing I've ever experienced, Jess. And yes, I'm obsessed. I want to know who and why. Thank you for worrying about me; you'll have to agree I could lose a couple pounds. Right now I don't know what I'd do without you."

"Okay, Maggie. I'm with you, you know that. But you have to let the police do their job. They have ways of finding out things."

"I know the police are doing everything they can, but Ron said there were no fingerprints and the killer left nothing behind. Whoever did it was very careful," Maggie explained.

"Sure," Jessica interrupted. "They were wearing gloves, probably those disposable kind that you get at the drugstore. I use them to do housework to save my nails." Jessica held up her beautifully manicured nails for Maggie to see.

"That's why I think someone saw something and maybe they will tell me but not the police. Let's go, I want to talk to that Ann again."

"Maggie, I want to eat my salad. I'm hungry! Good grief, take it easy. I'm not going to leave this twelve-dollar salad just sitting here. You can wait until I've finished or go it alone."

Maggie ate the rest of her salad in silence, then called the waitress over and asked for the bill. "I want to go upstairs again and look around the area where I found Mary. Maybe I'll remember something when I get up there," she told Jessica.

"Okay, okay, the things I do for my friends," Jessica said as they left the dining room. They took the escalator to the second floor. Maggie caught her breath as she looked toward the ballroom. She fought back tears as she walked to the loveseat that had held her friend's body just a few weeks before.

"This is where I found her. She was sitting right here in this very spot. It looked like she was just sitting there resting. I sat down beside her and started talking. When I touched her she didn't move and she was so cold."

"Maggie, stop! You're too emotional. You have to get hold of yourself. Stop thinking about Mary and try to remember if there was anyone else here. Look around. How was the furniture arranged? What about that doll? There was a big old doll sitting just over there when we came and when we left it was gone."

"The doll was in the ladies' room when I went looking for Mary. The doll belonged to Rita. She was quite upset when she couldn't find it." Maggie's mind was turning. "I think the doll was moved so no one would look this way. When you come out of the ballroom and face the chair that the doll was sitting in, you would look right at the loveseat where I found Mary."

"Did you tell Ron about the doll being moved?"

"I don't know, I can't remember. It didn't seem important at the time. I suppose Rita thought someone was playing a prank on her. Maybe she told Ron."

"I think you had better call Ron and tell him. It may be important."

Maggie hugged her friend. "You're right. I'll give Ron a call this afternoon, but I'm still going to have another talk with our little friend in the lobby. Nothing jogs my memory here and it looks like they've done a thorough job of cleaning, so we might as well go."

"Yes, I'm no help either," Jessica confessed.

They stepped off the escalator and almost bumped into Darlene Reed. When she saw Maggie she tried to make a hasty retreat but Maggie called out to her.

"Darlene, wait, it's Maggie. I've been trying to get in touch with you. I've left messages on your machine. Did you get my messages?"

"I don't think we have anything to talk about. You can call my family's attorney if you want. He'll be happy to talk to you."

"Why would I need to talk to your attorney? Mary wanted you to have your father's things. We can get together at the house whenever you want."

"It's not just his things I want. I want the house and everything in it. I'm entitled to it all since I'm Hank Reed's only child and Mary didn't have any children. So we will be seeing you in court, and maybe sooner than you would like if they charge you with Mary's murder."

Maggie's heart was pierced with those words. She knew Mary would forgive Darlene for all her nasty remarks but Maggie couldn't. How could anyone, even a stepdaughter, be so cruel? She had always known Darlene was spoiled but she was carrying this a little too far. Maggie loved Mary like a sister and she remembered how Mary always made excuses for Darlene. So she decided to hold her temper, at least for a while, for Mary's sake.

Jessica grabbed Maggie's arm. "Maggie, what did she mean, charge you with murder?"

"It's a long story. I can't talk about that now."

Darlene turned and stomped off, going through a door marked "Office." Maggie tapped on the door and entered. There was Ann, in the burgundy suit, and Darlene apparently discussing the conversation she had just had with Maggie.

Maggie stopped short. "What is this? Do you two know each other? Is this the reason you won't tell all you know about what happened, Ann? Darlene, if you had anything to do with Mary's death, so help me God I'll see to it that you pay."

"Don't threaten me, Maggie. I could cause you a lot of trouble. Like I said call my lawyer and leave me alone!"

It was suddenly clear to Maggie that Ann had been feeding information to Darlene about the events that took place the day Mary was murdered. But why? Why would Ann have an interest in Mary's death? She was just an employee of the hotel. Did she have something to do with Mary's death? But that didn't make sense. Nothing made sense—murder didn't make sense!

"Get out! Get out!" Ann shouted. "If you don't leave right now I'll call security."

Maggie was shaking. She wanted to say something more but knew it was best to just leave. She backed out of the door without saying another word. She took Jessica's arm and together they walked out of the Sommerset Hotel.

"Oh my goodness," Jessica said. "That Darlene is quite a little number, isn't she? Ann is too; I thought for a minute she was going to hit you with that letter opener. Did you see how she held it up like she wanted to strike you with it? I think she would have if you hadn't left when you did."

"Yes, she was sure filled with rage." Maggie shook her head. "I didn't think what I said should have upset her that much. I just want a few answers."

"Well she really scared me." Jessica shivered as she walked along. "That girl needs some anger management classes."

"Oh, that Darlene is such a brat! She was always so nasty to Mary. Well, she thinks she's getting the house, but Mary left everything to Becky," Maggie stated.

"Do you think her family lawyer will contest Mary's will?"

"Who knows, they have so much money already and you know what they say: 'The more you have the more you want.' The Andersons don't have the kind of money it would take to fight it out in court with Darlene's family. We'll just have to make that a matter of prayer."

Maggie gave the doorman the ticket to retrieve Frank's Mustang. Soon the young man drove up beside her with a big smile on his face. "No fingerprints, no scratches. Bring her back any time. I'll guard her with my life. Your husband is a lucky man."

"You bet he is," Maggie said, "and not just because of the car."

Maggie gave the kid a tip and eased herself into the Mustang. Jessica slipped into the passenger seat and snapped her seatbelt on. Maggie was still shaking as she shifted into drive, left the garage, and pulled into the street.

"Riding in this car with the top down is sure a lot of fun. I wish I had thought to bring a scarf, though. Don't you wish we'd had something like this when we were young and single?" Jessica yelled over the roar of the wind and motor.

"When we were young and single we couldn't afford something like this. I did most of my riding on the city bus."

"When I was young and single most girls didn't have cars of their own. These days, seems like as many girls have them as boys."

Suddenly something hit the back of the car. Both women's heads jerked back. Jessica let out a scream and turned around in her seat to see what hit them. The car jumped forward and sideways as Maggie tried to get control.

"It's a black Mercedes. I can't see the driver. The windows are tinted. Hold on! Here it comes again." Jessica was screaming and holding on to the back of the seat with her left hand and the dash with her right.

The black car hit the back of the Mustang again. It hit and pushed. The Mercedes's motor was roaring and its tires were spinning and smoking. Maggie was doing her best to keep control of the Mustang. There was a lot of traffic and she didn't want to put anyone else in danger. "I'm going as fast as I dare with all this traffic. Who is this nut? Someone's gonna get killed! Can you see the license plate? Get the number!"

"I don't think it has a license plate!" Jessica screamed.

The Mercedes kept coming, bumping the back of the Mustang, and pushing bumper to bumper, tires screeching. The downtown traffic was heavy and there were pedestrians waiting to cross at traffic signals.

"Thank God that light was green!" Maggie yelled as she pounded the horn, causing several women to jump back on the sidewalk out of the way.

The Saturday shoppers had their arms full of packages, some holding children's hands. Two teenage girls were eating something out of a small bag. A teenage boy made a hand gesture and yelled its definition, causing Jessica to blush.

"The driver of that car must be on drugs, and where's a cop when you need one?" Jessica yelled back.

Maggie saw an opening in the traffic and accelerated. "Hang on, Jess!" Taking a quick right turn, she headed down a side street, hoping to lose the black car. The black car squealed around the corner a little too fast and swerved into a parked delivery truck.

Maggie took advantage of the incident to make a few more turns, then she headed for the freeway on-ramp. She pushed down on the accelerator, causing the passing gear to kick in. The Mustang's 289 V8 engine roared and moved forward. Luckily, the traffic was light and Maggie was able to hit the freeway at full speed.

"I think we lost it," Jessica said, still looking over her shoulder. "You can slow down now. I don't like going this fast."

"Okay, but you keep an eye out for that black Mercedes. If you see it again, get my phone out of my purse and call 911 fast. Frank is going to be so mad. I dread seeing what the back of this car looks like."

"I had a bad feeling about this. Taking Frank's car to town was a big mistake."

"Too late now, Jess. The damage is done and you have to be with me when I face Frank." Maggie drove past Jessica's house and into her own driveway. "By the way, are you all right? That car hitting us really jerked us. I think we need to report this and then we both need to see the doctor just to be safe."

"I feel all right now, but I'm still shaking. That was really scary. Yes, I think we both need to see the doctor after we face Frank."

They both walked around to look at the back of the car. Just then, Frank came out of the house. "What's going on, Maggie? Where have you been?"

"You weren't home after the parade. You took my SUV and I wanted to go to lunch at the Sommerset."

"So you took the Mustang to town. What are you looking at?" Frank asked. He walked around and looked at the back of the car. "Now how did that happen, Maggie?"

Maggie told Frank all about the black Mercedes chasing them around town.

"I'm so sorry, Frank. I know this car is your pride and joy. I shouldn't have taken it to town, but I wanted to go back to the Sommerset and talk to that Ann. I'm sure it was her in that car. She was so hateful when we talked to her."

Jessica interrupted. "It could have been Darlene. She was pretty threatening, too. The way she acted I wouldn't be surprised if she was in on it."

"Let's not worry about that now. I need to drive both of you to the emergency room and have a doctor look at you. We'll worry about the car later and I'll talk to Ron about filing a report with the police."

Chapter 8

Ron Waters walked across his yard and up the walk to the Coppenger front door. He stopped to admire the bright pansies that outlined the flowerbed in Maggie's front yard. He was always amazed at how perfectly manicured Frank and Maggie kept their yard without any outside help. Maggie, sitting on the living room sofa engrossed in her latest mystery, jumped when she heard the doorbell ring.

Who could that be? she wondered as she opened the door. "Ron, come in. What a nice surprise. I was hoping to hear from you."

"I was just admiring your yard. How do you keep it looking so beautiful? I never see a weed in your flowerbed and none of those nasty little dandelions in your lawn."

"We both manage to get out there and do a little every day. You've got to keep ahead of it, otherwise the weeds take over."

"Yeah, like they're doing to my yard. Anyway I thought I'd better stop by to see how you're doing after your bumper-car incident. Are you all right? Sounds to me like your snooping around is getting on somebody's nerves. I want you to stay out of this. Whoever killed Mary is not playing around. You could get hurt real bad."

"I know, Ron. I already got the lecture from Frank. But it just seems like you're not making any progress."

"Listen, we're following up on some leads. Just because we haven't arrested anyone and I don't tell you everything I know, doesn't mean we're not doing our job. Remember Maggie, you're still the prime suspect, so you had best keep a low profile. I had to do some fancy talking or you would be in jail right now."

"Ron, you know I didn't kill Mary. Why would you even think that?"

"You were there, you had blood on your hands—"

Maggie interrupted. "I know, but don't you think if I had killed her I would have been gone before anyone saw me?"

"Yes," Ron reassured her, "but the captain doesn't like to have unsolved murders on the books, and the mayor's up for re-election. So I'm telling you to stay home and stay out of this."

"Okay, I promise. But you had better promise me that you will get the person responsible for Mary's death. You know it's not me. She was my dearest friend."

Ron put his arm around Maggie then held her at arm's length. With his hands on both her shoulders he looked into her eyes. "We'll get the person responsible, I promise. Sometimes it just takes time. This is real life. It's not like those TV shows where the police share everything they know with the amateur lady sleuth and the bad guys spill their guts and the crime is solved before the clock chimes the next hour. Gathering evidence that will hold up in court, talking to people that don't want to talk to us—it takes time, Maggie. Don't give up on me. It isn't going to be easy getting through this. There's usually a reason for murder. You may find out some things about Mary you'd rather not know."

"Jessica said the same thing. She thought maybe Mary was growing marijuana under her roses or had some deep, dark secret."

"Well, I can assure you there's no marijuana under her roses," Ron said.

"I've known Mary since we were both in kindergarten. She would never be involved in anything illegal. You know how you're always saying if everyone lived like Frank and me—law abiding, church going, patriotic—that you'd be out of a job? Well, you can include Mary in that. If anyone lived by the golden rule it was Mary."

"Maggie, I'm just saying, whoever killed Mary did it where there were a lot of people around. They were careful to cover their tracks. They had a reason for killing her."

"A reason? What reason could anyone have to kill Mary? She was so sweet. Mary never knew a stranger. She would have struck up a conversation with anyone. Anyone that knew her wouldn't think anything weird about her talking to a stranger. No, I'll never believe there was a reason to kill Mary."

Ron was trying to get through to Maggie about the danger she was in. He knew she was not a murderer, but someone was, and they had dragged Maggie into their web of violence. Ron was afraid for his dear friend.

"Mary and I had some real heart to heart conversations," Maggie said. "If she stumbled into something unsavory, she sure didn't let on about it to me. She cared about people. She did everything in her power to make this world a better place. There was nothing evil or deceptive in Mary's character."

* * *

Maggie woke early the next morning. She went into the kitchen and started the coffee. The sun was shining through the window. Birds were hopping around the lawn, poking their beaks into the ground. Some pulled up long, wiggling worms, and others were probably eating seeds and bugs.

What a beautiful day. How could this happen to me? How can anything so horrible and ugly be facing me on this beautiful day? Out loud Maggie said, "Dear God, help me to get through this. I need to know who killed Mary and see them brought to justice. I don't know if I can get through this without going crazy." The coffee finished brewing and the aroma drifted to Maggie's nose. She filled her cup, took a sip, and savored the strong flavor.

"Good morning, Maggie," Frank said as he planted a kiss on Maggie's head. "Sounds like you're talking to God. From what Ron tells me, God's the only one that knows who the killer is."

"I'm depending on Him to bring that person to justice. Help yourself to the coffee. I'm going to have some French toast. Can I fix some for you?"

"Sounds good. I'll spend my morning in the garage if you need me."

A second cup of coffee, French toast with apricot jam, and Maggie was feeling like she could face the day. After the bed was made and she was dressed she put her makeup on and used the curling iron on her short hair. Maggie's heart was sinking. "Is this how it feels to be depressed?" she asked herself. "I don't want this to happen to me but all the evidence points to me. Could I have killed Mary? No! But I could be charged with her murder. Ron is the only person that stands between me and jail.

"I've got to get on with my life, at least for the time being." She checked her posture in the mirror. "Mom, I got all your good genes. Thanks. At least so far my bones are strong and my hair hasn't turned that mousy gray. Inheriting good genes is a lot better than inheriting money. But it would be nice to have some of Rita's skinny genes." Maggie was talking to herself; it was her way of sorting things out.

The doorbell rang and Maggie went to answer it. "Rita, come in. I was just thinking about you. I'm going to make my morning shake. Will you join me?"

"Sounds good, let me help. We need to talk about the Red Hat fashion show that's taking place next month. I really need your help," Rita said as she entered the house and followed Maggie to the kitchen.

"Rita, get two glasses and that measuring cup from the cupboard. We'll sit out on the patio and drink our shakes."

Maggie went to the refrigerator for the ingredients. "I put bananas in the freezer and get these packages of frozen berries. One frozen banana and one cup of frozen berries, one cup of yogurt and one cup of orange juice. Put it all in the blender and in a minute or so you have a shake." Maggie turned on the blender and the two women watched the whirling mass of fruit and yogurt until it became smooth and creamy. Maggie poured the mixture in two large glasses and handed one to Rita. Then they walked outside and sat on the patio swing.

"This is delicious. I'll have to make this myself sometime." Rita took another sip. "What's Frank up to this morning?"

"Frank's in the garage with his cars. He'll be busy out there all day."

"We need to talk about the fashion show. It will be held at the Sommer Town Mall. All the department stores and some of the boutiques will be furnishing clothes, shoes, hats and jewelry, and whatever else strikes our fancy. The models will be our own Red Hat ladies. The mall will be doing a lot of advertising so attendance should be good. The best part is that all the stores have agreed to give the models a big discount on anything they model."

"Sounds like a lot of fun. I talked to the owner of Jackie's Boutique. She didn't know about the Pink Hats so I had to explain that they are the Red Hat wannabes, or women under fifty. Anyway, she's pretty excited about the whole Red Hat thing. She has ordered a lot of purple outfits, and a few in lavender, and some very exciting hats in both red and pink. She even has a few purple hats for those special occasions. Which reminds me, Frank and I have an anniversary coming up before long."

"Have you planned anything to celebrate?"

"No, this whole thing with Mary has taken the joy out of any celebrating. So I think we'll just let this one slide by."

"Getting away for a few days might be good for you. Have

you talked to Frank about it?"

"Let's just get on with the fashion show."

"Okay, Maggie, just a suggestion." Rita was beginning to be a little concerned about Maggie; she was usually so polite and caring, and this wasn't like her. It had been several months since Mary's death. "I just want to help. You're my friend and I'm concerned about you."

"I know, Rita, I'm sorry. I've been short with everyone. Jess and I were almost killed a couple days ago by some lunatic trying to run us over downtown. Then Ron told me again yesterday that I'm still the prime suspect in Mary's murder. The mayor's up for re-election and the captain doesn't like unsolved murders on the books."

"I didn't hear about you and Jess getting run off the road. When did this happen?"

"After the parade I took Frank's Mustang to the Sommerset. We had a run-in with Darlene and that hostess, Ann, at the hotel. Then on the way home a black Mercedes kept ramming the back of the car. I was finally able to lose them."

"Oh my goodness, Maggie! What did Frank say? Was his car hurt? Did you go to the police?"

"Yes, the car was scratched and dented. Frank didn't say a cross word. I think he was afraid he would say something he'd be sorry for. The car's still in the shop."

"What about the police? Did you report it to the police?"

"Yes, Frank went next door and got Ron to look at the car and we told him what happened. We filed a police report, but since we couldn't get the license number of the other car there's nothing the police can do. I'm sure it was that Ann. We tried to ask her some questions about what she saw that day; it was like there was some evil being possessing her."

"I'm so sorry. You must be crazy with worry over this whole thing. What can I do to help?"

"That's why I said let's just get on with the fashion show.

I need something to occupy my mind. Ron ordered me to stay out of it. So back to the fashion show! Are you finished with your shake?" Maggie asked as they walked back into the kitchen where she put their glasses in the dishwasher. "What about Pink Hats, how many do we have?"

"There's about a dozen Pink Hats in the group and they are all gung-ho. Several want to model. I think they will add a little extra excitement to the show. Some of the outfits I've seen will go very well for women outside of the organization. Here's the schedule: the Singing Sisters will do two numbers, the first one to start off the show and the second one at the end. Marie Reader is their soloist. I think she used to sing professionally. I met her once briefly, she is real sweet, reminds me of Mary," Rita said.

"Yes, I met her at the gathering. Milly introduced us," Maggie said.

"The manager of the mall, Phil Wallace, wants to be involved. He will welcome everyone and introduce the fashion show. I will be the moderator for the fashion show," Rita explained. "I'd like you, Jessica, and Susan to help the models behind the screen when you're not modeling yourself. We need to keep the traffic behind the screen to a minimum. Things can get pretty confusing back there if there are too many people. You gals will have to help the models so they won't look like they've been thrown together when they come out on the runway. It's a real fast pace and gals that have never modeled can get easily frazzled."

Maggie smiled and said, "I know, but I want to model, too. Jessica and Susan said they won't model. We can handle everything backstage; I'll be the last one to model."

Maggie took the schedule and looked it over. "This looks like a full afternoon. We will have to keep things moving to show all the outfits. We don't want any of the stores to feel slighted. It's so generous of them to supply all these things, even jewelry."

"Maggie, how's the investigation going? Has Ron said any more about who they suspect killed Mary, other than you?"

"No, he tries to keep me informed as much as he can, but he can't share much. He said they're following up on some leads. The police even went through Mary's house, but they were careful and didn't mess things up."

"On TV they always trash a house that they search," Rita said.

"Ron assured me that real life isn't like TV. Everything looked normal. They were very careful. Thank goodness."

Rita leaned over the kitchen counter. "I still think the mystery woman knows something. If we could find her we would find out something. I asked everyone I could think of and no one knows anything about her. I wonder if the hotel had a security camera in that area. Maybe we could find her that way."

"Ron already asked the hotel security about that," Maggie said. "They said they didn't have any cameras in that part of the hotel. But it was a good thought."

"No security cameras; that's convenient for someone committing murder," Rita observed.

"Well, you can understand that. Guests in a hotel don't want to be spied on. It's not like a bank or a store where there is merchandise," Maggie said.

"Oh sure, I understand, but it would have been nice to have the whole thing on camera," Rita said.

Maggie agreed. "If you had the murder on camera we wouldn't need a witness and you wouldn't be wracking your brain trying to find the mystery woman."

"The fashion show is coming up and I'll be on the lookout for her. She wore a red hat, so maybe she's a member of one of the groups. I'll recognize her if I see her again."

"Let's hope she shows up. We could use a break. I just

can't bear the thought that someone will get away with murder, and I don't like this black cloud hanging over me," Maggie said.

"We will find that mystery woman and we won't stop until we find her. I promise."

"Thanks, Rita, I know I can count on you. I'm pretty excited about the fashion show. I haven't thought about anything much since Mary's death. Getting dressed up and modeling some new clothes could be just the thing to get me out of the dumps. You know me when it comes to clothes."

"Yes, you and me both. I think this will be good for all of us."

"Rita." Maggie sat down hard on a chair at the kitchen table and began to turn the centerpiece around with both hands.

"Yeah?" Rita sat in the chair next to Maggie.

Maggie's eyes filled with tears as she turned to face her friend. Rita put her hand on Maggie's and gave it a little squeeze.

"Rita, Ron said I'm the prime suspect in Mary's murder. The day Mary was killed, that sergeant was about to arrest me when Ron came. If it hadn't been for Ron I would have been arrested! I don't know how I'd survive in prison."

"Oh Maggie, that's crazy! What motive would you have for killing Mary?"

"I was there and I had blood on my hands. It seems that's enough to make a case. Ron advised us to get a good criminal lawyer. Frank and I went to see one that he recommended."

"I'm so sorry! You must be half crazy. How is Frank taking all this? I can imagine he's furious; he's so protective of you."

Maggie broke down and cried. Rita put her arm around Maggie's shoulders and gave her a hug. She wondered how this would all turn out. She couldn't imagine her dear friend in jail.

Chapter 9

Maggie was at Jackie's Boutique two days before the fashion show, trying on some of the outfits Jackie had ordered for the occasion. She finally settled on a lovely purple dress with a flowing skirt, a modestly low-cut neckline with flowers made of rhinestones that cascaded down to the dropped waist.

"I feel like a queen in this dress." Maggie pointed to a hat tree. "I think I'll try the hat with the big brim. I love the veil. It gives a bit of mystery to the ensemble. What do you think?"

"You look smashing, Maggie. You'll be a hit," Jackie said as she moved around her, taking in the entire ensemble.

"Thanks for letting us model your terrific clothes in the fashion show. I want to buy this whole outfit," Maggie said as she twirled around in front of the mirror.

"I'm delighted to have my fashions modeled by the Red Hat ladies; it's good publicity for the boutique. After all, it was you who introduced me to this Red Hat thing."

"I'm always talking about the Red Hats. It's such a big part of my life. All my friends are Red Hat ladies."

"Well, you must have a lot of fun because the ladies that come into the shop are always in a good mood. Even when they don't purchase a thing I enjoy having them come in."

"We love the search for a new outfit. Most of us have a wardrobe full of red and purple so we're usually not in a panic for something new. But of course we are thrilled to find something that fits our figure and our budget."

"Look at this pantsuit, Maggie, you would look great in it. It's your size, too," Jackie said as she held up the hanger with the pantsuit on it.

"I like it," Maggie said. "A girl can't have too many purple outfits, now can she?"

Jackie picked up a red beret. "This would look great with the pantsuit. Try it on." Jackie held the beret up with one hand and twirled it around on her fingertip.

Maggie looked at the beret and the smile left her face. "No, Jackie, I couldn't. Mary was wearing a beret just like that one when she was murdered. She had a rhinestone hatpin in it and they said that is what the murderer used to kill her."

Jackie quickly put the beret back where she got it. "Maggie, I'm so sorry, I didn't know. Now that you mentioned it I think I remember her buying it here."

"It's not your fault. It's just that the police haven't arrested anyone yet. I don't think they've made any progress in their investigation and I can't forget how horrible it was finding her. I don't think I will ever be able to get it out of my mind. I think I'll just stick with this one outfit; I'm out of the mood." Maggie didn't tell Jackie that she was the prime suspect in Mary's murder. That she was only free and walking around because Ron had stepped in just in time to save her. She thanked God for Ron and prayed something or someone would turn up and solve this murder.

"I understand, Maggie." Jackie took Maggie's selection to the checkout counter. Jackie spoke slowly, with a slight European accent. She was a petite beauty, whose dark brown eyes flashed as she spoke. She wore her hair pulled straight back in a tight chignon. A simple black dress and a single strand of pearls gave her an air of elegance.

* * *

When Maggie had first stepped into Jackie's Boutique she was impressed with the quality and the variety of the merchandise. Their personalities had clicked right away; Jackie was the kind of person Maggie wanted for a friend. With the Red Hat craze in full swing, Maggie suggested Jackie bring in some red hats and purple outfits along with some accessories. "I'll bring my Red Hat friends in," Maggie promised. "I think you will have a hard time keeping up with their demand, once the word gets out."

At first, Jackie had been a little skeptical. "Red and purple, that's not exactly a wise fashion choice." However, when Maggie and her friend Rita wiped out Jackie's meager selection of purple and red items, Jackie decided to place an extra order just to see what would happen. She dressed one of her windows with red hats, purple clothes, and all the boas and purses the window would hold. She designated one corner of the shop as the purple and red corner. As soon as the display was finished, Jackie called Maggie.

"Maggie, I took your advice. My shipment of red and purple fashions has just arrived. My girls are hanging things in the purple and red corner as we speak and I can't wait for you to see the window display. The red and purple with a little pink and lavender is very exciting."

"Jackie, that's wonderful! I can hardly wait to see it and do a little shopping. My Red Hat friends need a shop they can count on for those casual and sophisticated outfits I know you will have on hand. You will love the Red Hat ladies, they have worked hard all their lives, raised their families, and now they are ready to enjoy life and have a lot of fun."

* * *

Maggie was thankful for the diversion of the fashion show. It was just what she needed to get her mind off Mary's murder. She had been consumed with the events of that day, the day Mary was murdered. Maggie kept going over things in her mind, hoping to remember some little detail that might help. Did she see something or someone? What was she missing? Maggie had heard that you see things and your subconscious mind remembers but your conscious mind doesn't always remember. So maybe, if she kept trying, something would come to her. She couldn't stand it if whomever killed Mary got away with it, and why would anyone murder Mary? She was the kindest person Maggie had ever known. She was always helping people, and she never had a bad word for anyone.

* * *

There was a good crowd waiting to see the fashion show. Two hundred chairs had been set up in the mall's center court. Most of the chairs were filled with women. Small groups of teens clustered here and there and a few men lingered, enjoying the music. To the right of the runway a band was playing jazz. Behind the screen that hid the models from the audience, racks of clothes made the space a tight squeeze. Nametags were pinned on all the garments with a number indicating the order they were supposed to go on stage. Plastic bags covered each garment, and they hung on rolling racks. There were other plastic bags attached to the hangers. One bag contained the hat and other accessories, like scarves and jewelry. Another bag held shoes and purses. Each hanger contained a complete outfit that had been chosen by the model herself. The stores had gone all out to make this show a real success.

Rita went fluttering backstage, checking to see if all the models were ready to go. "Maggie, we're ready to start, is everyone here? Come on, let's do it." Rita twirled around and bounded up the stairs to the stage runway. She gave Phil Wallace a nod and handed him the battery-powered microphone.

"Ladies and gentlemen, welcome to the Sommer Town Mall's Red Hat Fashion Show. All the models are from the Red Hat clubs right here in Sommer. The clothing and accessories have been furnished by our own boutiques and department stores. They are available for you to purchase today at our special Red Hat Fashion Show sale. Follow the program you find on your chair, so you will know where you can purchase the fashions. The band you've been listening to is Danny Brown's Jazz Band. Now let's hear from the Singing Sisters." Phil clapped his hands as he backed out of the way.

The Singing Sisters came bouncing onto the stage. They were all dressed in bright purple '20s-style flapper dresses. Their red headbands had feathers on one side. They looked as if they belonged on a movie set with Jean Harlow. The crowd loved them, clapping and whistling as the Singing Sisters left the stage.

"That was sure fun," Marie Reader said. "Thank goodness not one flash from some newspaper's camera."

Rita stepped forward as the Singing Sisters left the stage. "They'll be back a little later. Aren't they great? Now, let's get on with the fashion show!"

Rita introduced each model and identified their Red Hat chapter as they came on the stage. She described the outfit they were wearing, giving credit to the store that provided each item. At first the ladies felt a little awkward since most had never modeled before, but before long they were really getting into the spirit of it. They were coming onto the stage, strutting down the runway, twirling and posing. Several ladies that had big feather boas used them to twirl overhead or drag them behind in the style of the Paris models. The drummer in the jazz band did drum rolls. The crowd clapped and whistled. Everyone seemed to be having a good time.

Phil Wallace was feeling the excitement, too. His job as mall manager depended on successful sales. He needed events like this to bring people into the mall. Since women did most of the spending, this was the perfect event. He decided he would have these Red Hat ladies do this again next year. It could be an annual event. Phil knew a good thing when he saw it

"Our last model is Maggie Coppenger from the Mystery Mamas Red Hat Club. Maggie is wearing a sassy looking dress just right for that special evening out on the town. Bright red ostrich feathers and graceful netting that comes down over her eyes make this hat a real winner. Maggie has chosen earrings to match the rhinestones on the front of the dress. Her purple beaded purse really sets this outfit off. Jackie's Boutique furnished this entire ensemble."

Maggie walked down the runway with her best model's walk. *I'm not as slim and trim as those New York models but right now I feel like one. As a kid I secretly wanted to be a beautiful fashion model. Yes, I can do this!* Stopping at the end of the runway for a short pause, then a turn, she headed back up the runway. Hearing the applause and a loud whistle Maggie felt excitement rush through her. Instead of walking off the runway she stopped and turned again; the skirt of the dress swirled around her legs. Maggie paused and held out both arms, giving the audience a big smile and a wave before she turned to leave the stage.

As Maggie left the stage the Singing Sisters ran on. They began singing and doing a little dance that was half Charleston and half cancan. Danny Brown's Jazz Band played along with them. The crowd, noting the fashion show was over, began to thin out. Some of the younger people gathered around the stage, singing along, and a few started dancing with the music. At the end of the song, the Singing Sisters gave a bow. The crowd started yelling for an encore. Danny gave a nod to Marie and started playing the same song again. The Singing Sisters gave it all they had.

Out of breath but still smiling, Marie said, "I'm too old for this fast pace. If we have to do encores we'll have to learn some slow steps."

The Singing Sisters waved to the crowd and left the stage. Phil Wallace thanked Rita and asked if she would like to make the fashion show an annual event.

* * *

As Maggie passed Rita to leave the stage, Rita grabbed her arm and whispered, "Maggie, she's here. You remember the gal that was at the gathering. She's sitting out there, next to the last row, red hat."

"I'll go see if I can talk to her," Maggie whispered back. Maggie walked off the stage and found Susan and Jessica. "We really wowed them," Susan said.

"Yes, it was fun. That mystery woman is here; I'm going to see if I can catch her. I need you to cover for me back here."

"Go ahead, see what you can find out, we'll be fine," Jessica said. Susan nodded her head in agreement.

Maggie was feeling the excitement of the fashion show and now the prospect of finally, hopefully, talking to the mystery woman. Would she provide some clue as to what happened the day Mary was murdered? Maggie spotted her, and trying hard to control her emotions, walked slowly toward her. The woman's hands were in her lap; she was sitting alone and holding the program from the fashion show. Now and then she turned her head, looking back over her shoulder as if she was expecting someone. She looked very small and insecure sitting there alone. She was wearing a purple sweater, slacks, and a very stylish red hat.

Rita's right, she doesn't look old enough to wear red. She's barely in her twenties if that old, just a kid. This beautiful young woman couldn't possibly have anything to do with Mary's murder. But maybe she saw something. This should be very interesting, Maggie thought as she approached the young woman.

"Hi, I'm Maggie Coppenger, I noticed you sitting here alone. May I sit down for a minute?"

"Hello. Yes, of course, no one is sitting there. My name's Kate Bennett." Kate Bennett had a lovely smile, blond hair, and big blue eyes. Her complexion was smooth and clear, and she wore very little makeup. Maggie could feel her sweet gentle spirit and knew at once that she liked this young woman.

Chapter 10

When Kate was sixteen years old, she lived the life of a normal teenage girl. She was outgoing and was very popular at school. Her brother John, ten years older, had already graduated from college and was an engineer working for a large firm in the heart of downtown Sommer. Kate idolized her big brother and he took that responsibility very seriously. When Kate's parents were killed in a car crash, she was overcome with guilt and grief. She thought if she had done something different she could have changed the outcome.

Kate was at school when the word of her parents' death came. The principal and the school nurse broke the news to her. The shock of their sudden death caused Kate to collapse in a seizure. She was rushed to the hospital where she was kept under observation for several days. Her only living relative was her brother John. Determined to give her the proper care, he sent Kate to a small private boarding school. Her parents' death left her scarred emotionally, but after a while she was able to return to her high school. Kate's friends didn't know how to treat her after she returned to school. They still wanted to be friends but in her quiet world of guilt she somehow managed to turn them away. Kate graduated from high school and enrolled in college because she knew that's what her parents would have wanted.

* * *

"Kate, I'm happy to meet you. I think you were at our Red Hat Spring Gathering at the Sommerset Hotel." Maggie shook Kate's hand and held it for a long minute.

"Yes, I was there," Kate said nervously.

Maggie noticed that the mention of that day at the Sommerset triggered something in this young woman. Obviously she knew something. Maggie was determined to pursue it. She had to find out what it was that Kate knew.

"I wanted to talk to you then but everyone was so busy and then I couldn't find you. An awful thing happened; one of our Red Hat ladies was murdered. Kate, did you by chance see what happened?"

"Murdered? Oh no! A Red Hat lady was murdered? You mean the little lady with the white hair?" Kate began to wring her hands. "Murdered, a Red Hat lady was murdered?" Kate asked again and she began shaking and started to stand.

Suddenly Maggie felt concern for this girl. Her eyes held no malice; there was only a soft sadness in them.

"It's all right, Kate, no one will hurt you. You're safe and you're not in trouble. I just want to ask if you saw anything that might help us find the person that killed her. The little lady with white hair, her name was Mary. She was my best friend."

"I think I saw what happened. I was so scared. There was this person, she was talking real hateful like, she looked real mean and I think she hit the little lady!" Kate started talking faster and began to fidget in the chair. "I saw her take the doll away, at first I thought it was a real lady but it was just a doll. I followed her into the ladies' room so I saw that it was just a doll. But the old lady, she was real, all right. I heard them talking and then I think the younger one hit her, the older one. Then she left real fast, she walked away real fast! I should have stopped her but I got scared and went to find Johnny and told him I wanted to go home. I'm sorry, I could have stopped her. I could have yelled for help, I could have checked on your friend. Maybe I could have given her CPR or something. If I had done something your friend wouldn't have died. Just like Mom and Daddy. If I had done something they would be alive, too." Kate began to cry, real tears flowing down her cheeks. Her shoulders slumped, she seemed so small and fragile.

Maggie looked in her handbag for her hankie; she took it out and handed it to Kate. "Please don't cry. It's not your fault and you might have put yourself in danger." Kate took the hankie and wiped her eyes with it. "Do you know who the younger person was? Have you seen her again? Who is Johnny?" If Kate really saw what she just told her, Maggie finally had some hope of finding out who murdered Mary.

"Johnny? He's my brother. He brought me here, he'll be back soon. He went to the bookstore. I'm really not comfortable talking about murder."

"It's all right. Murder is a very nasty subject and I'm glad to hear you're not comfortable with it. I'll wait with you until your brother comes."

"I saw you model up on the stage. Your dress is real pretty." Kate wanted to change the subject and think about something pleasant. All this death and murder talk brought back sad memories of her parents' death.

"Yes, I like it too," Maggie told her. "Jackie, the owner of Jackie's Boutique, let us model some of her clothes. I liked this dress so much I went ahead and bought it. It was a lot of fun. Maybe next time we have a fashion show you could be one of the models. Do you think you would like to model?"

"I think I'd love it," Kate said, smiling at the idea.

"Kate, tell me about the person that hit my friend Mary. Anything you can remember will be helpful. Mary was my best friend. We first met in kindergarten. We grew up together and I can't stand the thought that whoever killed her could get away with it. They need to be caught and brought to justice. Please try to remember, did you hear what they were talking about?"

Since her parents' death, when something unpleasant happened Kate would try to block it out of her mind. She wouldn't watch the news on television or read the newspaper. There were too many unpleasant things being reported that she couldn't cope with.

Maybe I could make a difference. Kate tried to remember. *If I could help Maggie find the person that killed her friend, maybe, just maybe, I could make a difference.*

"I remember your friend, Mary, said something like, 'I don't know what you're talking about' and 'that's not who I am,' something like that." Kate was digging deep into her memory. She closed her eyes and pressed her fingers to her temples. Then she looked at Maggie. "It's like the young woman thought Mary was someone else and she was really mad at her," Kate said thoughtfully.

Maggie could tell that Kate wanted to help but she was getting upset. Kate's brother John came and stood by her and put his hand protectively on her shoulder.

"Katie, are you all right?" he asked. Then he turned to Maggie. "I'm John Bennett, Kate's brother. Kate seems to be upset; is there a problem?"

John Bennett had a nice build, about five foot ten, maybe six feet tall. He was wearing a pale blue golf shirt and tan slacks. Maggie thought he was as handsome as his sister was pretty. His short, wavy blond hair and clear blue eyes were warm and caring when he looked at his sister.

"Hello, John, I'm Maggie Coppenger." Maggie extended her hand. "Kate and I were just talking about the Red Hat Fashion Show. I was one of the models."

"Katie enjoys this Red Hat stuff." John patted his sister on the shoulder, then shook Maggie's hand. "It's nice to meet you. Kate, are you ready to go?"

Maggie didn't want Kate to leave for fear she would never see her again, and she hoped Kate could provide the clue as to what happened to Mary. "John, please wait, Kate may have seen what happened to my friend, Mary Reed. She was murdered at the Sommerset Hotel. We were at a Red Hat event and it seems you and Kate were at the hotel that very day. Kate thinks she remembers something and maybe it will help the police in their investigation." Maggie was about to panic when John took Kate by the hand, helping her to her feet. "John, please!"

"Maggie, it's nice to meet you but Kate has had some emotional problems and she gets confused when she is pressured. I'm concerned about her getting involved in a murder. I don't want her to get upset again. Besides, it sounds dangerous," John said as he put his arm around Kate and tried to move her away from Maggie.

"Johnny, cut it out! You're always worried I'm going to flip out again." Kate pushed her brother away with a firm hand. "I know you love me and you mean well but we're talking about murder here. I'm pretty sure I saw that woman kill Maggie's friend at the Sommerset. Dangerous or not, if I saw a murder happen, do you think I could live with myself if I didn't tell all I know?" Somehow Kate felt she could vindicate herself if she was instrumental in bringing a murderer to justice.

"Okay, okay. Just calm down and let's talk about it." John sat down on one of the folding chairs. "What do you think you saw?"

"Okay, remember when we were at the Sommerset and you went into the bar to watch the game on the big-screen TV and I went up to where the Red Hats were meeting?"

"Sure I remember. You came running into the bar acting all upset, saying you wanted to go home right now! It was halftime so I drove home and finished watching the game at home."

"Right, well I never told you why I was upset and why I wanted to get out of there." Kate looked him in the eye. "I saw something, I saw this young woman abusing this old lady. I should have yelled and called for help but for some reason I was frightened and just wanted to get out of there."

"If she did kill that lady, it is a good thing you left right away. She might have come after you. Your instincts are always good—do what your instincts tell you," John told her.

"Well that's easy to say but it has bothered me all this time and now that I know what probably happened, I'm ashamed." Kate lowered her head.

"There's nothing to be ashamed of. I can tell you are a wonderful, caring person," Maggie tried to reassure her. "All you need to do is tell what you saw and I'm sure if you describe the woman the police will be able to track her down."

* * *

Kate looked at Maggie, who she knew was older than her mother, but Maggie was a Red Hat lady and Kate knew her mother would love to be in Maggie's Red Hat club. Kate felt comfortable around Maggie. She wished she wasn't so shy; she kept everything inside. *Oh how I wish I could get up there and model. I could do it! I could walk like those models on TV. No, I couldn't. I'm not pretty and I'm afraid. If only Mom was here with me. It would be such fun. I could do it if Mom was here cheering me on. I'm wearing your purple outfit and red hat, Mom. Remember the first time I borrowed your blue sweater and it fit me perfectly? After that I was always sneaking into your closet and borrowing something. I remember you would just smile and tell me to be careful because it was your favorite. We drove all the way to Sandpoint, Idaho, to shop at Coldwater Creek. You bought that beautiful outfit, the one you were wearing when you and Daddy left, the last time I saw you. Oh, Mom, what am I going to do? I'm all alone. Johnny is great but he doesn't understand. He's so afraid something will happen to me. He's sweet. Did you know he even wanted to take me to the prom? Of course I told him no!*

A group of us from church went, boys and girls. Oh, all the girls would have been happy if he had gone with us. They all swoon over

Johnny, they think he is so handsome, of course he is.

But he's so much older than any of my friends and he thinks of them like he thinks of me, his sweet little sister. Mom, I miss you so much. I miss Daddy, too. I'm sorry for all the mean and hateful things I ever said to you. I hope I can help this nice lady find the person that killed her friend. I just can't believe I may have witnessed a real murder. Mom, if you're up there looking down on me, please help me. Help me to be strong and remember I love you.

Chapter 11

The fashion show was over and most of the spectators had left the area. The Red Hat models were behind the stage gathering up the fashions they had modeled, getting them ready to return to the stores that loaned them. Everything had gone as planned. The Singing Sisters were a great hit singing with Danny Brown's band, which played off and on throughout the show. The models were the local Red Hat ladies that had little or no experience but soon they began to walk the runway with a stride that took on the air of professionals. The audience seemed to have a good time; they clapped and whistled when one of the models strutted down the runway with a little extra wiggle in her hips. Phil Wallace was delighted. He felt sure it would be a great shopping day with so many excited women in the mall. He had worked hard on this event, organizing a huge advertising campaign with television and newspaper ads. The band hadn't come cheap, and setting up the seating area, stage, and sound system required extra workers, so Phil was depending on the stores making a good profit.

Kate said she saw the woman that had hit Mary, maybe her killer, and she was here.

"Kate, you said she's here, the person that hit and killed my friend Mary. Can you show me where she is? Do you see her now?" Maggie pleaded. *Oh God, let it be so. Let her be here so we can identify her. Thank you for sending this beautiful girl to me. Thank you for her brother John. Bless them, Lord, please.*

"She's here, I saw her. Let me look around, maybe I can find her again." Kate got up and walked around the outside perimeter of the seating area. She stood there for a short time, and then suddenly started walking fast toward the stage. "There she is, Maggie! Come on, I see her!"

Kate was a sweet, innocent young girl and the thought of hurting an old lady was unthinkable to her. Now that she realized she had witnessed the murder and she could identify the murderer, she was eager to help. She had been frightened the day she saw it happen. Even though she didn't realize Mary had been killed, she had felt there was something terribly wrong and the person that hit Mary was someone to be feared. Now with Maggie and Johnny beside her she mustered her courage and was determined to stop this evil person. Johnny always tried to protect her but this time she wouldn't let him stop her. She liked Maggie and if Mary, the lady that died, was Maggie's friend, then Kate would do everything she could to find her killer.

Maggie took off after Kate as fast as she could go, with John right behind her. "Katie, wait!" John raced past Maggie. "Katie, wait for me!"

Kate ran up to the woman that had just come from behind the stage where the models changed clothes. The woman looked to be in her late twenties, with long blond hair, about five feet two inches tall. There was hardness to her features; she was slim in tight-fitting jeans and a tank top that showed tattoos on both her arms. Kate blocked the woman to stop her from leaving the area. The blond took a swing at Kate but Kate saw it coming and raised her arm, blocking the blow. The blonde was moving fast and the impact of her body sent Kate sailing backward. Down she went, hitting her head on a nearby chair. Kate got to her knees and was a little dazed; she shook her head and reached for the blonde's leg as she moved past.

"What's the matter with you? Can't you see I have a gun and I'll use it?" the blonde yelled as she pushed past Kate. "Stupid—!" The blonde added some obscenity that Kate couldn't hear.

"Stop her, Johnny! Stop her! That's the one." Kate sat on the floor, a little disoriented, but she continued to yell. "You've got to stop her!"

John ran over to Kate, looking her over for blood and bruises. "Are you okay? I saw her push you. Are you okay, Katie?"

"I'm okay. That was her, Johnny! She looks different but it's her, I'm positive! She's got a gun and she said she would use it. Call 911." Kate sat up, rubbing the back of her head, then she scrambled to her feet. Looking around, she grabbed John's hand and pulled him. "Come on, we've got to stop her."

"No, Kate! That's enough. If she's got a gun we're through. I want a doctor to look at your head. Then we will go home," John said sternly. "I think you've had enough excitement for one day."

"It was pretty exciting, wasn't it Johnny? But someone has to stop her, she has a gun and she might kill someone else. We can't let her get away."

"Don't worry, Katie, the police will get her."

Someone must have alerted mall security. Three security guards in navy blue uniforms came running into the area, a look of confusion on their faces.

"Over here!" John yelled as the female security guard approached. "I need a doctor to look at my sister. That crazy woman pushed her and she fell backwards."

The guard was already talking into her handheld radio. "I've already called 911. The paramedics should be here soon. We got a call from Phil Wallace, the mall's manager. Have you seen him?"

"You have to stop that crazy woman. She has a gun!" Kate yelled at the guard.

Two paramedics carrying cases that contained their emergency equipment came walking into view, and John waved to get their attention.

"Be still, Katie, the paramedics are here. I want them to check you over."

"Johnny, I'm okay! We have to help Maggie get that blonde. She's the one that killed Mary. We have to stop her!"

* * *

Phil Wallace heard a commotion behind the screen and went to investigate when he tripped over Marie Reader. He fell right on top of her, getting blood all over his hands and the knees of his suit pants. A blond woman leaning over Marie had blood on her hands, too. She was startled as Phil practically fell on top of her. She gave him a shove with both hands, then kicked him, knocking him away from her. He grabbed at her but she struggled away, then jumped up and started running. Phil took out his cell phone and hit the automatic dial for mall security.

"Security, get down here, call an ambulance! Some crazy woman attacked me and one of the singers!" Marie looked bad. Phil called her name and patted the side of her face but got no response.

"I'm sorry, Marie, but I've got to stop that woman." He got up and stepped over Marie, following the blonde as she went running from behind the screen.

Phil yelled, "Stop her, she just attacked Marie Reader!"

* * *

Marie was hurting. Her mind, foggy and confused, tried to focus on what just happened. She had been attacked from behind. Someone grabbed her and jerked hard, flipping her whole body around.

"What are you doing?" Marie cried.

"Don't you remember me?" The woman held Marie tight. Some demonic presence seemed to be staring at Marie through the woman's eyes. "Sure you remember me. I swore I'd get even with you if it was the last thing I ever did, Marie Reader!"

A sharp pain sliced at the side of Marie's shoulder and down her arm, bringing with it a sensation of something hot moving over her. Then the hot turned to freezing cold. She dropped to her knees and collapsed on the blood-covered floor. Someone called her name; she tried to answer but she was drowning in blackness.

As the blackness engulfed her, Marie struggled with images that floated through her mind. There was a beautiful, dark-haired child surrounded by big, ugly men. A young woman with long black hair and eyes like burning coal danced around Marie's body, but she wasn't Marie. That wasn't her name. What was her name? She couldn't remember. The woman danced around, stepping on Marie's body—flames shot from the woman's eyes. Marie was burning, but at the same time she was freezing. She felt her life slipping away. Who was she? What was her name?

* * *

Just as Phil yelled, the blonde turned and pulled a gun from her shoulder bag and shot at him. The bullet grazed his left arm, ripping through his clothes, tearing at his flesh. The pain was intense and sent him spinning. He went down, hitting the floor hard.

"Oh God, I'm gonna die." Retching with pain and nausea, Phil struggled to get control. His mind was slipping away—suddenly everything went black.

* * *

Maggie heard the shot and saw Phil go down. "Oh my God, it's Phil!" Maggie pleaded to heaven as she looked for Kate. A woman with long blond hair was moving fast toward the girl. The blonde pushed her and Kate fell backward. *That's her,* Maggie thought, *I've got to stop her! God help me.*

The security guards seemed to be moving in slow motion

and there were no police anywhere in the area. Maggie knew she had to do something or Mary's killer would get away. She would leave the mall and there would be no hope of catching her and bringing her to justice.

The blonde turned again after firing the shot that hit Phil; as she did, she bumped into a row of chairs where two boys were sitting.

"Hey, watch it!" one of the boys yelled.

"Creep," the blonde said as she pushed him out of her way.

"She's got a gun! Oh man did you see that? She's got a gun!"

"Yeah, look, she shot that guy. Get down, keep low."

"Oh man, when my mom hears about this she won't let me come back to the mall ever again. She's always afraid I'll get into trouble."

"Bet she never thought about you getting shoved by a lady with a gun."

"Lady, she's no lady. Did ya hear her call me a creep?"

Maggie felt herself getting angry again. There was a rage swelling up inside her and she knew the only way to put it to rest was to stop this person. Just then the blonde rushed toward her; Maggie took a good hold on the strap of her purple beaded handbag.

"God help me!" Maggie yelled. "If that's her, stop her, stop her!"

Maggie swung the handbag with all her might and hit the blonde square on the side of her head. The blonde threw her arm up and grabbed at the purse, yanking it hard.

Maggie fell into her, then grabbed hold of her and held on tight.

"Let go of me!" The blonde jerked sideways trying to throw Maggie off.

Something urgent possessed Maggie and she gave the

blonde a hard karate chop on the side of her neck. The blonde staggered and crumpled to the floor. Maggie threw herself on top of her, holding her down. The blonde was on her stomach, kicking and screaming, struggling to get free. Maggie straddled her back and held on tight, refusing to let go.

"Somebody, help me!" Maggie screamed. "I don't want to hit her again but I will!"

Determined to keep the woman down, Maggie pulled her hair and with a sudden jerk, off came the blond hair. "A wig!" Maggie screamed.

The gun that the blonde had just shot Phil with went sliding across the floor near where John was sitting with Kate and the paramedics.

"Don't touch the gun! Fingerprints!" the paramedic yelled at John as he quickly bagged the gun. John grabbed a roll of duct tape from the paramedic's bag, then quickly approached the blonde and pulled her arms behind her and wrapped the tape around her wrists. She began to struggle, screaming and cursing, throwing Maggie off balance. John straddled her knees and used the tape to bind her feet at the ankles.

"If you don't shut up I'll tape your foul mouth shut," John told her as he helped Maggie up. "Maggie, are you okay?"

"I'm fine! I can't believe what just happened. Did I karate chop her? I must have looked like a crazy woman." Maggie laughed as she straightened her dress.

"You did and you looked great," John said.

"You really got her." Kate was laughing as she ran to Maggie and gave her a hug.

"Thank you, Kate, we make quite a team."

"We sure do, I spot them and you take them down!"

"You were pretty good yourself, the way you blocked her with your arm. That was a good defensive move," John said, beaming at his sister. "If you hadn't raised your arm when you did I think she would have hit your face with that gun."

"Yes, and I think I'll have a bruise on my arm to show for it." Kate grinned as she rubbed her arm.

"Better your arm than your face," Maggie said as she lovingly patted the side of Kate's face.

Phil pulled himself up, feeling lightheaded but glad that he was still alive. One of the paramedics helped him to a chair. "Did someone stop that mad woman with the gun?" Phil asked.

"She's over there on the floor," the paramedic told him. "The police will be taking her into custody."

"I wish someone would have got to her before she shot me," Phil complained.

Just then two uniformed police officers walked into the area. "What's going on here? We got a report of shots fired," one of the officers said as he took out his notebook and began making notes.

The paramedics found Marie behind the screen and quickly went to work on her. She had lost a lot of blood and was not responding. Her pulse was weak. They stopped the bleeding and started an IV, then put her on a gurney and rushed her out of the mall into their waiting ambulance.

Milly Good couldn't believe what was happening. When she saw the paramedics taking Marie away she ran after them.

"Wait, I'm coming with you," Milly yelled at one of the men. "I'm the only family she has."

"All right, but you'll have to sit quietly," he said.

"Thanks, I'll be quiet. I just need to go with her." Milly waited for the paramedics to put Marie in the ambulance, then she climbed in. She sat quietly praying all the way to the hospital.

Maggie walked over to one of the police officers. "Please, will you call Lieutenant Ron Waters of homicide? He's in charge of the Mary Reed murder investigation. I'm pretty sure this is the person that killed Mary. She attacked Kate here and she shot Phil Wallace, the mall manager. She and I had a little scuffle and John Bennett, that's John in the chair, managed to tape her hands and feet so she couldn't get away." Maggie was breathless. She had used all her energy. A wave of satisfaction flowed over her, but she was still trembling. The beautiful dress Maggie had modeled in the fashion show was ruined. It was torn up the side, and the rhinestones on the front were hanging down, ripped away in the struggle. Tears came to her eyes as the reality of the situation hit her full-force. The strength left her legs and she collapsed on a nearby chair. Emotion gushed from deep inside her. Covering her face with her hands, she sobbed quietly.

Phil Wallace sat on one of the chairs wishing he was anywhere but here. He pulled at his bloody pants leg. "She tried to kill Marie Reader. She was bending over Marie and there was blood all over the place. I caught her in the act and she tried to kill me too," Phil said as he grimaced at the paramedic who ripped the sleeve of his shirt to reveal where the bullet had grazed him. "Ouch! That really hurts!"

"It's just a scratch. It could have been a lot worse. Luckily it didn't hit bone, but you're going to the hospital anyway. You need a tetanus shot and maybe some antibiotics, but you'll live."

"Yeah, it may look like a scratch to you, but I've never been shot before. And I don't like it. This was supposed to be such a great day. No one's going to do any shopping this afternoon, shots fired, police all over the place. What a mess! Look at my suit. I'll probably lose my job over this, too."

The two boys came up off the floor, looking around to make sure it was safe.

"Good, the cops are here."

"Wow, that was something, was you scared?"

"Yeah, kinda. I never was in a shootout before. Let's go see if we can find out what it was all about." The boys walked over to the officer that was taking notes.

"Hi officer, what happened, did she rob a store or something?"

"Did you boys see what happened? What are your names?" The officer had his notebook and pen ready to take down information from any witness he could find.

"I'm Joey Martin and this is my friend Todd Blackwood. We were just sittin' over there. We heard a shot and that lady ran right into us."

"We saw she had a gun so we stayed out of her way." Todd pointed to the woman that the other officer and security guard were standing over.

"Good thinking, boys, never mess with a person who has a gun. Are either of you hurt?"

Todd said, "I'm okay. She just gave me a little shove is all."

"Yeah, I'm okay too," Joey said. "Did she rob a store or something?"

"I don't know, son, but she's in big trouble, whatever she did."

"Can we leave now? We were waiting to get into the movies when the shooting started."

"Sure, go on, I've got your names. Tell your folks what happened because someone from the police department might come to your house to talk to you. Enjoy the movie." The officer waved them away.

Maggie kept looking at the woman lying on the floor. She couldn't understand her emotions. Maggie wanted to hate her, but laying there on the floor with her hands and feet taped she was a pitiful looking sight.

"Who is this woman, anyway?" Maggie asked as she walked over to the woman, thinking she looked familiar. "She was wearing a wig. I think I know her!"

* * *

Lieutenant Ron Waters arrived on the scene. "What on earth

is going on here?" he asked one of the uniformed officers.

"Lieutenant, this lady asked me to call you. She said it was about a homicide you are working on. That little bundle on the floor there just tried to kill several people. We've got a witness that says she was seen attacking your Sommerset Hotel vic."

"Thanks, Sarge. Did you get statements from everybody?"

"Still working on it, lieutenant; they rushed one off to the hospital in pretty bad shape. Paramedics didn't know if she would make it."

Ron Waters raised his hand. "Just get their statements. It's gonna be a long day," he said as he walked toward Maggie. "Okay, Maggie, what happened?"

Maggie introduced Kate and John to Ron. Together they filled him in on the events that lead to bringing down the woman that was lying on the floor. Phil Wallace told Ron about the blonde attacking Marie and shooting him before the paramedics took him to the hospital in a waiting ambulance.

Finally, Ron instructed two of the uniformed officers to take the woman to headquarters. "Get her out of here! Read her rights, and then book her on suspicion of murder and at least two counts of attempted murder."

The woman was kicking and screaming obscenities as the officers lead her out of the mall. One of the officers was reading her rights over her loud wailing.

Chapter 12

Sandra Malone sat at her father's desk remembering a happier time. A time when the whole world was beautiful and exciting, and her future was bright with promise; now her future was uncertain. Sandra's mother had died many years ago. Now her father was lying in a hospital bed, paralyzed from a stroke.

What if he didn't recover? Would he be like this forever? What if he got worse? What if he died? No, I have to think positive! He's my only family. He will get better! He will come out of this. I'll move back home, I'll be here for him, I'll make sure he gets better. I'll leave my job. When you're better, Papa, I'll get another job, but right now I'll stay right here, close to you.

Already Sandra had taken a leave of absence and agreed to fill in for her father at his office where he kept the books for a chain of nightclub restaurants. Sandra would do anything for him, anything to keep him from worrying. The office was small and dingy, in a bad part of town. She was thankful for the parking space right by the entrance that led into the building in the alley behind the restaurant. How could her father spend so much time in this dreary place and not get depressed? But then he was never aware of his surroundings. How many times had Mama mentioned painting the kitchen or living room or getting new curtains? His response was always, "It's fine!" Sandra remembered how once her mother had been so proud—she had painted the kitchen herself and made new curtains for the window over the sink. Finally, after three days she asked him what he thought. Without looking up from his morning paper he said, "It's fine." She went into the bedroom and quietly closed the door; when she came out a little later her eyes were red and swollen, and Sandra knew she had been crying. "You were always gentle, Papa, I don't ever remember you raising your voice. You never missed a day at work, and at the end of the week you gave your paycheck to Mama, only keeping a few dollars for yourself. You were a good provider, a good husband, and a good father."

Sandra remembered her happy childhood. She was very talented, with a beautiful voice, and she loved to sing. Sandra was an only child. Her father was always busy and her mother was very protective of her. In high school she was in the choir and drama classes. Her parents allowed her to enter talent contests as long as her mother was right there with her. She won almost every contest she entered but when winning meant she would have to travel out of town for the next event her mother always found an excuse so she wouldn't be able to attend. She remembered her mother's sweet voice.

"No, Sandra, we can't go, it's too far. Your father can't take off work and we can't go alone. Besides, it's too expensive."

She would argue with her mother knowing she couldn't win.

"But Mama, we don't need Papa to go with us, we could go alone. We could stay in a hotel and it would be like a vacation for you."

"No, Sandra, that's final, and don't ask again!" Mama's word was always final.

Oh Mama, if only you were here now. You and Papa were so protective of me. I know it was because you loved me so much. Papa saw what some of the club singers were like and he didn't want his daughter to end up like them. Oh Mama, how I miss you. You worried that I'd end up like those club singers. I just wanted to have some fun.

I'll never know if I was as good as everyone said I was. It was just a dream, that's all it was, it was just a dream.

After her mother passed away Sandra had tried to stay close to her father to fill the empty spot in her life. He was silently mourning the loss of his wife and seemed to think of nothing else but his work. Arthur was a bookkeeper, and numbers always made sense to him. Numbers were safe; he could cope with them. With numbers there was no confusion, no chaos.

Sandra buried her dream of becoming a singer in the back of her mind. College and her studies filled her life. A degree in business gave her a position with a large manufacturing company. This was definitely not what Sandra wanted as her career but she had bills to pay and she didn't want to ask her father for any more money; he had paid for her college tuition and all her expenses.

Sandra's father, Arthur Malone, was a bookkeeper for a chain of restaurant nightclubs that were owned by Carlo Martini. Some said Martini was connected to the mafia but no one had ever proved it and Arthur didn't believe the rumors. Carlo Martini treated Arthur like family, and at his age Arthur knew that good paying jobs were hard to come by. He kept the books in order, advised his boss on financial matters, and never asked any questions. He wondered what he would do if he ever found out that Mr. Martini was into anything illegal. What you don't know can't hurt you!

Sandra tried to get home to see her father at least once a month for a Saturday or Sunday visit. She begged him to come to visit her. She had a beautiful apartment in an upscale neighborhood with plenty of room for him to spend the night. Sandra thought it would do her father good to get away from his work and the neighborhood. But of course he wouldn't leave. His boss, Mr. Martini, might need him. He jumped every time Mr. Martini called. He was afraid of losing his job. Sandra knew her father couldn't compete in the job market. He was an old-fashioned man, the corporate world was looking for sharp young minds, and Arthur didn't look the part. He had a brilliant mind and when it came to finances he could work circles around his younger counterparts. Arthur was comfortable and set in his routine. He wasn't accustomed to traveling away from his neighborhood and his familiar surroundings. He didn't own a car but the neighborhood he lived in was close to everything he needed. He walked to and from work, even in the icy-cold Chicago winter. On the rare occasion he needed to leave the neighborhood he would take a taxi. Once in a while Mr. Martini would send a car and driver to pick him up. That usually happened on weekends or late at night when Martini had some business dealings at the club and needed to know something about his finances for some big deal he was working on.

"Art, how is that little daughter of yours?" Carlo Martini asked. "Is she coming home for Christmas on her school break? I'll bet she's all grown up now."

"Oh, Mr. Martini, Sandra has been out of school for several years. She has a good job as a bookkeeper," Arthur explained. "She lives about an hour from here. She's coming to spend a week with me at Christmas. I can hardly wait; it's been a long time since the two of us spent Christmas together."

"She's a bookkeeper, huh, just like her old man! That's good! I remember she used to like to sing, all the time singing. I told her when she grew up she could sing in my club. Do you remember that, Art?"

"Oh, sure I remember, Mr. Martini, but she has a good career as a bookkeeper. I don't think she has much time for singing these days," Arthur said proudly.

"You tell her hello for me, maybe she comes to the club with you at Christmas, I'd like to see her again," Martini said.

Two weeks later Sandra arrived at her father's house. She had come prepared to spend the week with him. She was hoping they could spend some quality time together. It had been a long time since they had really sat down and had a good visit. Even on her regular trips she didn't spend much time with him. It took most of her day to clean the bathroom, change and launder the bed sheets, and remove uneaten food left in the refrigerator from her last trip. She would check the pantry and do a little shopping, then prepare dinner, always making enough so her father would have some leftovers that he could warm up for another meal during the week. Sandra didn't mind doing those things for her father, she just wished he would take time to relax and enjoy life.

"I've got a whole week to spend with you, Papa. Let's go shopping for Christmas presents and trim the tree just like we did when I was a little girl. I'll cook Christmas dinner like Mama used to do. I found all her recipes. We can talk about old times and get to know each other again." She knew it was painful for him, talking about her mother, but at the same time it was good for both of them.

"Yes, Sandra, that sounds good. We will spend some time together."

"Papa, you and me, we are the only family we have and I don't want to forget Mama. I remember she was so beautiful and sweet. I know you miss her as much as I do."

Sandra wanted to spend the day shopping. Mr. Martini needed Arthur at the club. As usual he was working on another business deal and wanted the accounts up to date so he could have the figures in front of him.

Carlo Martini was a generous employer. He would give Arthur a list of names and beside each name was a number. Arthur would go to the office safe and take out one-hundred-dollar bills to match the number written by the names. Martini gave each of his employees a Christmas gift, always cash. No one was overlooked, from the waiters and bartenders that worked in the clubs to his personal assistants, which were really bodyguards. Carlo Martini treated his people well and he demanded respect and loyalty in return.

Since her father was busy, Sandra decided to use this opportunity to shop for gifts for her coworkers and her neighbor's children. She bought a soft gray cashmere sweater and a Sinatra CD for her father. She decided on Barbie dolls for the neighbor's girls. *You can't go wrong with Barbie*, she thought. It was lunch time and she didn't want to eat alone so she went to the club hoping to have lunch with her father. The office door was shut so she knocked.

"Come on in, I'll be with you in a minute," said Carlo Martini.

"I was looking for my father. Is he here?" Sandra asked as she held the door open, not knowing if she should go in.

* * *

There was something about Carlo Martini that caused Sandra to feel uncomfortable in his presence and yet she was strangely fascinated by him. Her father seemed to jump at his every command. Everyone that worked for him seemed to have some kind of reverence for him.

"It is respect for my boss, the man that pays my salary, the man that paid all your mother's medical expenses and paid for the beautiful funeral when she passed away. Of course I jump when he calls me. How do you think you went to that expensive college? It was Mr. Martini that made it possible," Arthur had told her.

"Do you mean Mr. Martini paid my college tuition?" she asked.

"Every year he asked me how much it cost to go to college and that was the amount of my Christmas bonus. Your college is paid, Sandra. You never had to take a loan. I never had to borrow money."

"But Papa, you never told me. Why would he be so generous? It's like everyone is afraid of him. And you jump every time he calls. Are you afraid of him?" Sandra couldn't understand that kind of reverence.

* * *

"Sandra? Is that you, little Sandra? I haven't seen you for years. You grew up while I wasn't looking," Carlo Martini exclaimed.

"Yes, it's been a long time, Mr. Martini. I was hoping to have lunch with my father. Do you know when he'll be back?" Sandra asked.

"He's gone to the bank to make a deposit. He'll be back soon," Martini said. "Tell you what, the chef's here, I'll just give him a buzz and he can fix us something for lunch. I'm hungry, too. We can all eat here in the dining room." Before Sandra could protest Martini pressed a button on the desk intercom. "Danny, Art's kid is here. Fix us something for lunch, something nice. Art will be back in a while. We'll eat in the dining room. Oh yeah, some of that good wine, too."

Mr. Martini got up from the chair and walked around the desk. Taking Sandra's hand he said, "Let me look at you. You grew up to be a beautiful woman. Your father misses you a lot. He's always talking about his little girl. You should move back here close to him, he's not getting any younger, you know. A father needs his children close in his old age."

Just then Arthur Malone came into the office. Surprised to see Sandra there with Martini holding her hand, he stopped short. "What are you doing here?" he demanded.

Martini let go of Sandra's hand and put his arm around Arthur's shoulder. "She's here for lunch, Art. I asked Danny to fix us something nice. Come on, let's go into the dining room. I'm really hungry."

Carlo Martini was a perfect gentleman and put Sandra at ease during their lunch. He asked her about her work and bragged about his little granddaughter, Carla, who was named after him. By the end of lunch, Arthur started to relax, too, thinking maybe he was too protective of his little girl.

On Christmas morning Sandra was busy in the small kitchen preparing a ham for their dinner. The kitchen was just as it had been when Sandra was a child. She used her mother's pots and pans and the good china. A lace tablecloth graced the table in the dining area where Sandra lit candles, giving the house a festive atmosphere. She bought a pie at the local bakery; sweet potatoes were in a casserole, smothered with brown sugar and marshmallows, waiting to go into the oven. They had opened their gifts to each other. Arthur was wearing his new sweater and Sinatra was crooning in the background. Sandra was wearing the new jogging suit and wristwatch her father had given her. He promised they would watch the Audrey Hepburn movie after dinner. *Breakfast at Tiffany's* was her favorite and she had worn out her old video so Arthur thought she needed a new DVD. One of the waitresses had gone shopping for the gifts and Arthur was pleased with her choices. It promised to be a perfect Christmas Day when the doorbell rang.

"Who can that be?" Sandra yelled from the kitchen. "Are you expecting someone?"

"I'll get it," Arthur said as he walked to the door.

"Mr. Martini, what are you doing here? It's Christmas, is everything all right?" Arthur said as he held the door open and Carlo Martini stepped into the living room.

"Call me Carlo. Like you said, it's Christmas! I just came by to bring you and Sandra a little gift and wish you a merry Christmas. Where is she? I smell something good cooking."

"Come in, come in. Sandra's in the kitchen fixing a ham for our dinner. Sandra, come out here, Mr. Martini brought us gifts. Please, Carlo, sit down, this is a nice surprise."

"I can't stay long, just wanted to drop in for a minute. My wife is fixing a huge dinner. We have a house full of relatives."

"Merry Christmas, Mr. Martini. How are you this morning?" Sandra said as she came from the kitchen.

"Merry Christmas, Sandra. Please don't be so formal—call me Carlo. I brought you and your father a little Christmas gift. Your father works so hard for me and I don't give him enough to compensate for all the extra hours he puts in." Carlo handed Arthur an envelope and a box of Cuban cigars. To Sandra he presented a small box. "Go ahead, open it. My wife, Angela, picked it out. She said it was just the thing for a beautiful young lady."

Arthur looked in the envelope; it was full of one-hundred-dollar bills. "But Mr. Martini, this is too much."

Martini put up his hand to stop Arthur from saying any more. "You deserve it, you're the best bookkeeper I ever had. I don't know what I'd do without you. You keep me out of trouble with the IRS. Sandra, open your gift." Carlo was beaming as he watched her.

Sandra had been holding the beautifully wrapped box. She sat down and carefully eased the ribbon off the box. The name, Tiffany, was on the outside of the box. Sandra took in a deep breath at the sight of it. Slowly she took off the lid. The most beautiful bracelet she had ever seen lay before her eyes. She couldn't believe it and didn't know what to do or say. The little tag in the box read, "cultured freshwater pearls, sterling silver." She just sat there staring. "Mr. Martini, I don't know what to say. I really can't accept this, it's so extravagant."

"Of course you can. I've never given you anything. In all the years your father worked for me I never gave you a gift. I have a new granddaughter, the first girl in our family, so now I know why you are so special to your father. Don't disappoint my wife, she chose it special for you. Wear it and enjoy it. Merry Christmas!" Martini got up and walked to the door. "Art, enjoy your cigars!" He gave them a wave and shut the door behind him.

"Papa, I can't believe it, this bracelet cost him a fortune."

"Now you see what I mean. Mr. Martini is a generous

man, and his people return his generosity with respect and faithfulness."

* * *

Things were going well for Sandra. Her life was comfortable, she could afford beautiful clothes, her apartment was just the way she wanted it. She had recently purchased a new BMW sports coupe; it was her dream car. A coworker had gone with her to the car dealer and advised her in the purchase. They had dinner together on several occasions and Sandra hoped their relationship might turn into something serious. She had seen too many of her friends end up in bad marriages, so she was determined to take it slow.

Jason Williams was tall, blond, and handsome. He and Sandra worked for the same company but in different departments. They ran into each other from time to time. After a few encounters Sandra noticed that Jason was turning up more frequently. She usually spent her coffee breaks catching up on some reading, but now she watched the door hoping Jason would enter, and most days he did. Sandra still carried her paperback novel to the break room but lately she wasn't getting much reading done.

One morning as Sandra and Jason were drinking coffee in the break room Jason asked, "How's the car?"

"Great, I love it. I really appreciate your help. What they say about women and car dealers is true. There was a big change in his attitude when you came there with me."

"Glad I could help. Next time you buy a new car give me a call, I'll be right there."

"That will be a very long time from now. This one will have to last. I'll probably be old and gray before I get it paid for."

"Sandra, I know you love musicals, and I have tickets to *The Phantom of the Opera* this Saturday night. I was hoping you would go with me."

"Oh, Jason, *Phantom of the Opera*! I'd love to but I heard it was sold out weeks ago."

"My family has season tickets and every now and then they let me have a turn. Mom is an opera fan and she doesn't let go of her seat very often but she and Dad are on a cruise."

"I'll be forever grateful to your mother." Sandra's heart swelled within her. She was mentally going through her wardrobe. She would have to go shopping after work.

"Great!" He tossed his empty Styrofoam cup into the trash. "I'll get back to you on the time." Jason smiled to himself as he walked back to his office. *Life is good,* he thought.

His secretary, sitting at her desk, asked, "Well, what did she say? From that grin on your face and that tune you're whistling I'd say she said yes."

"Yes, I've got a real date with that beautiful little gal in bookkeeping. I'll need dinner reservations and flowers. Can you help me out with that?"

"Sure thing, boss, consider it done."

Sandra was dancing on clouds. Jason was everything she had dreamed of in a man, a husband; he just might be the one. His parents seemed to like Sandra and she liked them. Sandra had met them the first time at Jason's cousin's wedding and once she had been invited to their home to celebrate his birthday at a backyard barbeque. Both occasions were attended by many friends and family. The one time Jason met Arthur, Sandra's father, was at the opening of one of Carlo Martini's restaurants. Arthur had insisted that Sandra be there. It was a perfect time for them to meet. Sandra wasn't sure how her father would react to her having a date. Any time she mentioned a male friend, Arthur seemed to have a negative reaction. Each time Sandra chalked it up to her father being overprotective of his little girl. Arthur seemed to accept Jason at that first meeting; or was it the importance of the occasion that overshadowed the fact that she brought a man to meet him? At any rate they seemed to hit it off and later Arthur told Sandra, "Bring your young man home so we can get better acquainted."

"Papa, do you mean it? Did you really like Jason?"

"He seemed like a nice young man, and he had good manners. Sandra, I know that someday you will marry. I can't keep you my little girl forever."

"Oh, Papa, I'll always be your little girl."

"I know, but I'm getting older and I want to know that when I'm gone you will have someone to take care of you."

Sandra and Jason were taking it slow, developing a solid relationship while building their careers. Sandra wasn't ready to give up her independence; she didn't want the kind of life her mother had, living only for her husband and child. Her career was important to her. They had the rest of their lives. There was security in being a couple and still being independent.

One day Sandra received a call while she was at work. It was the hospital; Arthur Malone had had a stroke. He was stable and was asking for her. "He's not in any immediate danger but come as soon as you can," his doctor said.

Sandra went home and packed a few things, not knowing how long she would be needed. She told her employer she would probably be gone a week or two. As Sandra headed home she willed herself to concentrate on her driving. Thinking about her mother's long illness and finally her death, Sandra fought back the tears. What would she do without her father? "Please, God. Please, I'm not ready for this. I can't lose him. I know he misses Mama but I need him. Please, God, let him live, make him well." Sandra prayed throughout the hour-long drive. In her mind she had prepared herself for the tubes and machines that had been used when her mother was so ill, but when she arrived at the hospital, much to her relief her father was sitting up and was able to talk to her. He had some paralysis on his left side and his speech was affected. Sandra stayed close to him for the first week, afraid of losing him. What would she do without him? He was all the family she had.

One day while Sandra was sitting with her father, just after she had helped him with his breakfast, Carlo Martini came into the room.

"Sandra, I'm happy to see you. Arthur, I have an emergency. I need the payroll for my employees for all the clubs. I know you're not up to it yet, but I thought maybe Sandra could do the payroll. You could tell her how to do it. Sandra, you know bookkeeping. I don't want to hire someone from the outside. Let's keep it in the family. Will you help me?"

Arthur took Sandra's hand. "Sandra, you can do it. You know the system; it's the same one you are used to using. Remember we talked about how similar our systems were. All the information is in the computer. You can do the payroll in one afternoon."

"Yes, Mr. Martini, I can do it this afternoon. I'll call you, Papa, if I have any questions, but if it's the same system I shouldn't have any problems."

* * *

Sandra wondered what she was getting herself into. She had to do this for her father, but Mr. Martini didn't want to hire someone from outside the family. How long would it be before her father could get back to work? How many payrolls would she have to do?

"Get well, Papa, get well."

Chapter 13

Dr. David March was tall, handsome, and soft spoken. He sat in a chair next to Sandra. He never sat behind his desk when he talked to a family member about a patient. He knew the medical terminology that described his patient's condition and the formal setting of his office only caused them to agonize more about the situation.

"I'm going to let Arthur go home as long as there is someone to take care of him. If you can't work something out so he's not alone he will have to go into a nursing home."

"But in time he will be all right, won't he?" Sandra asked.

"I don't expect him to make a full recovery; the stroke was pretty severe. He'll be on medication and we'll start him on physical therapy right away." The doctor tried to reassure her.

"I'll work it out," Sandra said.

Sandra called her employer and explained about her father's condition. He was very understanding and told her to take as much time as she needed. Her assistant knew enough about the job to fill in for her. Sandra knew the girl could do the job with no problem, and would be thrilled at the prospect of a promotion if she didn't return. After several weeks Sandra realized she would have to move in with her father; there was no other choice. A nursing home was out of the question. It would break his spirit. If there was any hope for his recovery she needed to be right here with him, encouraging him, making sure he took his medication, ate a healthy diet, and completed his physical therapy. Sandra resigned her position, cleared out her apartment, and moved home to take care of her father. It was a difficult time for her. She loved her job; she had made good friends, but she loved her father and wanted to take care of him. She would adjust. Jason would have to understand, and he would have to adjust, too.

"Of course I want to be here, Papa, it's not a problem. When you are on your feet again I'll be able to find another job, meanwhile I'm here for you. Mr. Martini has been very generous. I'm on the payroll with full benefits, same as you. I couldn't be happier."

"Since there's nothing I can do about it, I'm very grateful to you and Carlo. I don't think I could stand being in one of those homes."

"Don't worry, Papa, you are staying right here. You can manage just fine during the daytime while I'm at work. That nice Mrs. Johnson will be here. She's going to do some of the housework while she's here. She said she likes to keep busy."

"That's good," Arthur said. "I hate housework."

"Me too," Sandra added. "I really like Mrs. Johnson. I think she'll work out fine."

"As long as she minds her own business," Arthur told her. "I'm not used to having a woman around, and I sure don't want a nosy one poking her nose in my business."

"The agency said she was very professional. You're not to worry about all this, it's going to be just fine. You need to concentrate on getting well. Work hard on those therapy sessions. The therapist seems like a nice guy."

"Yeah, he's good, he really gives me a workout but I like him."

"That will help you pass the time during the day and we can spend some time together when I get home. You're here if I need to ask anything about the bookkeeping and if you need me all you have to do is call. We'll get along just fine."

Sandra did call him, and would ask him questions about the bookkeeping. "Sandra, you really don't need my help with the bookkeeping, but I like it when you call and it is important for you to know the history of each account. I like to be able to keep up on what's going on at the office." Sandra would do anything to keep his spirits up so she called him with any question she had, no matter how small, and when she got home in the evening she filled him in on the events of the day.

Carlo Martini was genuinely concerned about Arthur. He had come daily to visit while he was in the hospital. Carlo made sure the hospital and the doctors provided everything that was needed for Arthur's care. Once Arthur was home, Martini was just as considerate. He paid Arthur weekly visits, asking his advice about business matters and spending a little time just visiting. He was impressed to know that Arthur was well informed about the business even while he was recovering at home.

"Art, we are lucky to have Sandra, she's a smart girl. She seems to be fitting in real good. The girl knows her stuff. When you come back to work I think we can keep you both on the payroll. I might buy another club downtown. I need to talk to you about it before I make a decision."

Arthur smiled a crooked smile, one side of his face not responding. "Sandra makes me so proud, Carlo. She's a smart girl. Yes, you are lucky she would come here. I think she liked her old job more than she let on. Anyway, I've been thinking, this stroke took a lot out of me. I'm getting too old to be working on the books. My mind's not what it used to be. We all need to face the fact that I won't be coming back to work."

Carlo patted Arthur on his knee. "Arthur, we'll do what you want. If you feel like you want to retire, that's good. You have plenty in your retirement fund, but I'd like to be able to come and talk to you about business matters. I value your judgment. I know Sandra is capable of handling the books, that's not a problem. But you know, talking man to man, about business. It's easy with a man, not so easy talking to a beautiful young woman. You talk it over with Sandra and let me know what you want to do. Is that all right with you?"

Arthur nodded. "Yes, that's good. I'll talk to Sandra. I've thought a lot about it and I think it would be best for everyone if I retire. You've been more than generous, Carlo. I appreciate it. Thank you."

Arthur and Sandra talked it over, and then Sandra went to see her father's doctor. Dr. March agreed that Arthur would not be able to work again. He felt it was the best thing for Arthur to face that fact.

"Get him interested in something. He needs a hobby, something he will enjoy and that will help pass the time of day. He mustn't sit around feeling sorry for himself," the doctor said.

That evening after the dinner dishes were cleared away Sandra sat down next to her father in the living room. He was watching the evening news on TV.

"Papa, I think it's a great idea for you to retire. But I'm not going to let you sit around watching soap operas all day long. You need a hobby. So what will it be?"

"You're right, those soap operas can make you crazy. I used to do a lot of painting when I was young. I think I'd like to find out if I can still handle a paintbrush. There's this guy on the television that paints. He's good."

"You used to paint when you were young? I never heard about you painting."

"It was a long time ago. For years, I kept busy with work, and your mother always had something around the house that needed doing, but now I can't do those things any more. Now I got time, maybe I can get some of my artistic juices flowing again. Anyway, if you would drive me to the mall there's an art store there. I'll get supplies and see what the old man can do."

"An art store? I never noticed an art store in the mall. You've been checking it out, haven't you?" Sandra was thrilled to see her father so excited. "I'm learning things about my father that I never dreamed of. What next? Okay, Papa, I'll get our jackets and off we go."

Arthur took up painting and was good at it. He seemed to thrive on the excitement that each new painting brought. He painted with the guy on the television.

He was learning new techniques, preparing the canvas, mixing colors; he was having the time of his life. In spite of his physical limitations, Arthur was developing into a very talented painter. Sandra would pick up his paints, brushes, and canvas on her way home from work. When his paintings were finished and dry, she would take them to the frame shop and have them framed. She was thrilled to see her father doing so well with the painting in spite of the fact that the paralysis hadn't improved in the years since his stroke. There were pictures on every wall in every room in the house. Sandra hung several of his landscapes in her office and he had given some of his favorite ones to Carlo Martini.

After Sandra moved back home, Jason called her often. He made several weekend trips to visit her and her father, hoping to rekindle their relationship. Sandra was overwhelmed with her father's condition and couldn't seem to reconnect with Jason. Before long Jason began to feel rejected and eventually gave up on their relationship. Sandra concentrated on her job and tending to her father's needs; he was her main concern. Arthur seemed to be doing so well and had developed such a passion for his art that Sandra consulted a gallery about showing his paintings.

"Sandra, I don't think I'm ready for anything like that, I'm just a guy that likes to paint. There's nothing special about my paintings."

"Papa, I took several of your paintings to the gallery and the people there think you are extremely talented. They are willing to show your paintings at no expense to you."

"I don't think I could stand the stress. I just want to paint and not have to deal with people. We don't need extra money.

My paints and canvases don't cost that much money that I have to sell them." Arthur was getting upset and suddenly began to use his brush to slash across the canvas he was working on.

"Oh Papa, I'm so sorry. It was just a suggestion; you don't have to do anything you don't want to do. You just keep painting and enjoying it. I'll tell the people at the gallery that your paintings are not for sale."

Arthur seemed to settle back into his routine and Sandra thought everything was all right. Then one day when she came home from work, her father was lying on the floor. His paints were spilled on the floor and the easel was on its side next to him. Sandra dropped the grocery bag she was carrying and rushed to her father.

"Papa, what's the matter? Speak to me, are you okay?"

Sandra took him by the shoulders and shook him over and over, but there was no response from him. His eyes looked to her, pleading. She grabbed the phone and dialed 911. While she waited for the ambulance she sat on the floor with her father's head in her lap. Tears filled her eyes as she stroked the side of his face and begged him to be all right.

It took about ten minutes for the ambulance to arrive, but it seemed like an eternity. The paramedics came into the house and checked Arthur over. They started an IV and said they needed to get him to the hospital immediately. Sandra rode in the ambulance with him, crying silently and watching her father's face. The paramedics notified the hospital and Arthur's doctor was waiting for them when they arrived.

"This looks like a bad one," Dr. March told her. "I'm not sure he will make it, Sandra. You need to be prepared for the worst."

Sandra sat alone in the cold hospital waiting room. Her body was numb and her mind was jumbled with confusing thoughts. Did she push him too hard about the gallery and showing his paintings? She thought it would be good for him—she was so proud of his art. Instead she might have put too much stress on him. She should have known her father was a simple man and couldn't stand that kind of pressure. She didn't know what she was going to do. "Papa, Papa, I can't lose you, you are all I have, without you I'll be alone. I'm so sorry."

A nurse walked by, and seeing Sandra crying and the way she was shaking, the nurse knew she could go into shock if she didn't calm herself. The nurse brought Sandra a blanket and a cup of coffee.

"The doctor will be out to talk to you again, but you need to calm yourself. You can't help your father if you make yourself sick."

"I know, but I'm so worried," Sandra told her.

"Let's put this blanket around you and drink this coffee," the nurse said.

"Thank you, I am cold. I left in such a hurry I forgot my coat."

"Have you had anything to eat?" the nurse asked. "I can get you something from the nurse's station kitchen if you're hungry."

"This is fine. I don't think I could eat anything, thank you so much. It was just such a shock, finding him the way I did when I got home from work. I don't know how long he lay there on the floor. He's my only family, he's all I have. I know I have to get control of myself. Thank you for being so concerned."

"Sandra, what's going on? The hospital called and said Art came in, an emergency!" Carlo Martini thundered as he approached Sandra with two hulking big men behind him.

"Mr. Martini, it's Papa." Sandra jumped to her feet, hugging the blanket around her. "I found him on the floor when I got home from work. I didn't think to call you, how did you know?"

"The hospital has orders to call me if any of my people come in. Do you need anything?"

"No, I don't need anything. Thank you for coming. I'm just so scared. What if he doesn't make it? I'll be all alone."

"No, no, you're not alone. I'm gonna take care of things. I'm gonna leave one of my guys here. Tony's gonna sit outside Art's room. If you need anything you tell him. He's gonna take care of it." Martini kissed Sandra on the cheek, then he walked away with his bodyguard following behind.

Three days later Arthur died. Sandra was by his side holding his hand. The doctor tried to prepare her for his death, but you can never be prepared for a father's death. Sandra was hurting and alone.

Carlo Martini made all the arrangements for the funeral. "Sandra, you don't need to worry about anything. I'm taking care of it."

Sandra's mind was all awhirl. Panic hit her hard—it was like when her mother died all over again, but this time she truly was alone. She had always wished for brothers and sisters but now she wished for anyone.

Carlo's wife Angela took charge of Sandra. She came to her house early the day of the funeral to help Sandra dress and see to it that she ate something. Sandra clung to her as if she were her mother.

"Mrs. Martini, you're so kind, I don't know how I'd manage without you and your husband. I feel so alone, I'm so scared."

"You and your father work for Carlo, that's family. We take care of our family. Carlo's sending a car to take us to the church, then we'll all go to the club for a nice dinner. Don't worry, Carlo is taking care of everything."

Sandra liked Angela Martini. She reminded her of her own mother. Fussing over her, making sure she ate. It was comforting having this sweet doting lady with her on the day she would bury her father.

The car arrived. It was a long black thing appropriate for

the occasion. The driver was the same one that had guarded Arthur's hospital room, one of Martini's men. He was a bodyguard, an errand boy that jumped when Martini said to. Mrs. Martini was watching through the living room window, and saw the car as it pulled up in front of the house. She took Sandra's hand and led her out of the house.

"Tony!" Mrs. Martini yelled. "Good, you're here on time. We don't want to be late."

Tony just nodded and held the door open for Sandra and Mrs. Martini to get into the backseat of the car. He closed the door, then got behind the wheel and drove to the church where the service for Arthur Malone was to be held. Sandra was overwhelmed with the number of people that attended. They were all dressed in black and came to give their condolence to her. Most of these people Sandra had never seen before but Angela Martini explained who they were and their relationship to her father and Mr. Martini. Sandra had never seen so many flowers in one place. She felt suffocated by the smell of flowers and the blur of hovering faces that surrounded her. After the service Sandra was escorted to the car again and driven to the cemetery for the graveside service. Her emotions were running wild; it was all she could do to keep from screaming. She was thankful that the Martinis had taken care of the details of her father's funeral. The service was beautiful. The words the priest said gave Sandra a reassurance that her father's life had been well lived. But she was alone now. In the midst of this crowd she was alone.

Carlo Martini had arranged for the lavish array of food and drink at the club where Arthur had worked for so many years. Now Sandra worked in the same office. She knew she had to be visible at the reception, but her heart wasn't in it so she sat in a chair against the wall. Mrs. Martini sat with her. After an hour at the reception, Sandra told Mrs. Martini she would like to go home and rest. Mrs. Martini pushed her way through the crowd of men that surrounded her husband.

"Carlo, Sandra needs to go home and get some rest. Have Tony get the car. I'll take her home."

On the drive home Mrs. Martini told Sandra, "We have a room for you in our house. It will be perfect for you. We will love you like our own daughter. We will take care of you. You know we never had a daughter. Boys, three boys, and grandsons. Well yes, now we have little Carla, our first granddaughter. But you are family, Sandra. It's not safe for a young woman to live in the city alone. Live with us, in our house where you will be safe."

"I couldn't give up my home, the house I grew up in. It's all I have left of my parents."

"We will talk about it later, Sandra, right now it's too soon for you to make any changes."

Mrs. Martini yelled, "Tony, I'm giving Sandra your number. If she needs anything she's gonna call you."

"Okay," Tony responded.

Sandra was relieved to be home; she needed some quiet time alone. Mrs. Martini offered to stay with her but Sandra insisted that she needed to rest and preferred to be alone. She thanked Mrs. Martini for everything she and her husband had done and assured her that she would be fine.

Sandra insisted, "Go back to the reception and make my apologies for leaving early. Everything was so beautiful. All the flowers, the music, it was all so nice."

Angela Martini stepped into the car and instructed Tony to drive her back to the reception. She would report to her husband what she and Sandra had discussed.

They've been so kind and so generous, Sandra thought. *But they seem to want to control everything. They even want me to live with them in their house. Maybe it's my imagination but they want to control my life. They did arrange for everything, it was all so lovely. I would rather have had a small service but I guess all those people wanted to pay their respects to Papa.*

Sandra curled up on the sofa with a blanket. What would she do now? She wished she wasn't an only child. If she had a brother or sister, even a sweet aunt or uncle, someone of her own, then she would have someone to lean on. Now Angela and Carlo Martini were her family. She looked around the small living room. Her father's chair was empty, the fabric worn. Suddenly the whole room looked dingy and old.

Sandra wasn't ready to sort through her father's things. She needed them close to her, needed to touch them, to smell them. After several days of aimlessly wandering around the house she called Carlo Martini. "I need to go back to work, I need to keep busy."

"Are you sure? You take all the time you need."

"No, I'm ready to work, it's too hard sitting around with nothing to do."

"You know I'm no bookkeeper, so I'm happy for you to come back. In fact I've been thinking that I'm not paying you what you are worth. I'm giving you a good raise. You'll see in your next paycheck."

"Mr. Martini, you've done so much for me. I need to arrange to pay you for Papa's funeral. It was so beautiful, so extravagant. I'm sure I'll have to pay it back in monthly installments. You can take it out of my salary."

"Sandra, don't be silly, that's what we do for family. I don't want to hear another word about it."

Sandra had no family and had lost touch with her old friends. Jason had married a childhood friend so she couldn't call on him. She had the home she grew up in, her mother's things, and her father's paintings. She contented herself with that.

Several years passed and Sandra settled into the routine of work again. Things were going well for her. Carlo was a wonderful boss, treating her like family and pretty much let her have the run of the office. She was always included in their family gatherings. She grew to love Angela Martini. She was like a second mother to Sandra. There were a few things that concerned Sandra about Carlo's business. Her father had told her that Carlo was a very private man and she should never inquire about his other business dealings—the clubs were her only concern. "Do your job and don't get involved in anything else," Arthur had told her.

Chapter 14

Carla Martini was the apple of her grandfather's eye. She was like a little shadow following him around. When he was at his desk Carla would sit on his lap. She brought her toys into his office and remained there while Mr. Martini took care of business.

Carlo thought his granddaughter was too young to understand what was going on as he conducted business, but Carla took in every word.

"Grandfather, some day I want to run the family business just like you." Carla was only ten years old when she told him. "I will tell those men what to do and they will listen to me because I'm Carla Martini, granddaughter of Don Carlo. They will respect me just like they respect you."

Carlo Martini was surprised to hear his granddaughter call him Don Carlo. He assumed that she must have heard one of his men call him that. He was foolish to think this young girl thought only of the dolls and pretty dresses he lavished on her. Carla's wish to be just like her grandfather possessed her every thought.

When Carla was eight years old she had celebrated her First Communion. In her beautiful white dress, all ruffles and lace, she was the perfect picture of innocence. After the ceremony at the church the family gathered at the Martini home where a banquet of food had been prepared. Carla was the center of attention. She insisted on a huge chair from her grandfather's study be placed in a backyard gazebo where her guests presented her with gifts. The guest had to walk up three steps to approach her sitting in the chair.

Carla was a perfect little lady; she smiled and thanked each person, allowing the adults to kiss her cheek.

When her brothers and cousins came before her she insisted they bow and kiss her hand. "Say God bless you, Dona Martini!" she told each one as they handed her their gift. They did as they were told in fear of Carla throwing a tantrum and they would be blamed for disturbing the festivities.

Carla asked for everything she could think of and she got it. On her fourteenth birthday Carlo was out of ideas; he had lavished her with everything he could think of. To solve the problem he gave Carla her own credit card. The sky was the limit. She could buy anything she wanted. For her sixteenth birthday she wanted her own car. Not just any car, it had to be a Corvette convertible. Carla's mother was at her wits' end. She felt like she had no control over her own daughter. She wouldn't listen to anyone except her grandfather.

"Carla, don't you think you should start out with something a little smaller?" her mother asked. "After all, you can't get your license until your birthday and you haven't been driving that long."

"Grandfather said I could have anything I want, and I want a Corvette! He always gives me what I want."

"Yes, I know he does. You take advantage of him. Besides, that is a very powerful car, and I'm not sure you have enough driving experience to handle it."

"Oh, Mother, really! Grandfather said he would take me to the dealer and I could pick out the one I want and he will have it delivered on my birthday. You have nothing to say in the matter."

Carlo loved his granddaughter. She was his diversion from the problems of his life. He thought he was protecting her. She would never want for anything. He didn't want his little princess to have to deal with the dirty life that he was in. He would get the business legitimate and Carla would be safe and have a beautiful life with everything she could ever want. Carla spent a lot of time at her grandfather's office.

"Grandfather, I want to learn the business from the ground up. Let me help out in the restaurant. I can help with ordering the food that is served and make reservations for the dinner guests. This is what I want to do. Mamma doesn't want me to hang around here as much as I do, but I think I can learn a lot about the business. Please, Grandfather, give me a job right here working with you. Maybe I could work with Sandra and learn a little bookkeeping. You know I'm taking bookkeeping in school." Carlo worshipped his only granddaughter. Everything she said or did was joy to him.

Carlo Martini informed Sandra that Carla would be her new assistant. At first Sandra was delighted to have Carla's help, but eventually Carla had her own ideas about how things should be done.

Carla had grown into a strikingly beautiful young woman. She had everything going for her. She was beautiful and intelligent, but she was also spiteful and vindictive. Born into a family of privilege, her father Vincent was the third son of Carlo Martini. Vincent had had two sons before Carla was born. His older brother Salvatore, or Sal, had three sons. Joey Martini was blessed with two sons. So when Carla was born, the Martini family threw a huge party to celebrate. She was the first girl in a family of boys.

"Boys are good, but they have to be tough. They need to learn the hard things in life, survival," Carlo said. "But a girl, girls are soft and delicate and need to be protected."

Growing up with two brothers and five older boy cousins, Carla had her own personal bodyguards. She was treated like a princess.

Carlo Martini was a devoted family man, a gentle and caring husband, father, and grandfather. He was the same to Sandra, treating her like a daughter. How could she ever believe he was anything but good?

Sandra worked late on several occasions and during those times she saw some strange men coming and going into Carlo's office. Taking her father's advice she never asked Carlo anything about the men. One evening after working late, Sandra left the office and stopped at the grocery store. She was planning to spend the weekend at home and her food supply was low. She parked as close to the store entrance as she could. She needed quite a few things and didn't care to spend much time in the dark parking lot. Inside the store she took her shopping list from her purse and gave it a quick glance. She pushed a shopping cart up and down the aisles, choosing fruit, vegetables, eggs, milk, yogurt, deli meat and cheese, and a loaf of dark rye bread.

"Hi Amy, how's it going?" Sandra greeted the clerk as she placed her items on the conveyer belt at the checkout counter. "You're looking chipper for this time of day."

"Hi, Sandra. I just got back from my dinner break. I'll be here until midnight when we close up. I won't look so chipper then. Doing anything special over the weekend?"

"I'm spending the weekend going through my father's things. I think it's time. I'm not sure what I'm going to do with his clothes. I'll probably give most of them to charity. I've been putting it off, really dreading it. But I'm going to do it this weekend."

"It's gotta be tough," Amy said as she told her the total of her purchases.

Sandra reached into her purse, but her checkbook wasn't in its usual place. She unzipped another compartment and it wasn't there, either. "My checkbook, I can't find it. I don't want to use cash; that will leave me short for the weekend. I'll have to use my debit card." She swiped her card in the machine, put in her four-digit pin number, and pressed the enter button. "I guess I'll have to go back to the office. I must have left it there.

The Hat Pin Murders

Good thing I didn't get ice cream. See you later, Amy."

Sandra and Amy had been in high school together. They weren't what you would call close friends. Amy was a cheerleader and one of the most popular girls in school, especially with the boys, while Sandra was quiet and more concerned with her studies. Sandra was in the choir and drama group, so she was in all the school plays. Everyone liked her but she wasn't one of the really popular girls. After graduation, Sandra went off to college. Amy married her high school sweetheart and had three children. Amy's husband worked in a local factory on the day shift. Amy got the kids—two girls and a boy—off to school, did a little housework, then laid down for a nap. She would fix dinner for the family, then leave for work at the grocery store as soon as her husband got home. It worked out well with one of them home with the kids all the time and they both had weekends off. It seemed like a hard life to Sandra, but Amy seemed to be happy.

Sandra drove back to the club. Her assigned parking spot was taken by a little red sports car. "Happy hour," Sandra said to herself. "I'll have to ask Carlo to put more floodlights up. It's pretty dark out here."

Sandra took her key from her handbag, expecting the outside door to be locked, but when she tried the knob it opened. Thinking Carlo must be working late, she headed for his office. As she approached his open door she heard loud, angry voices. She recognized Carlo's voice, and the other man sounded like a delivery man that she had talked to on a number of occasions as he delivered things for the club. Thinking better of it, she turned around and headed toward her own office.

I'll just get my checkbook and go home for a nice quiet evening and finish that book I've been reading. Her checkbook was on her desk where she had left it. She remembered that one of the waitresses' kids had been selling candles for a school fundraiser to earn money for cheerleader uniforms. Sandra could never resist when it came to kids. She had written a check to the girl's school for four candles that would be delivered to her in three weeks. Sandra loved to have candles around the house. She lit them any time she was at home; the fragrance and glow of burning candles gave the old house a cozy feeling.

A popping noise that sounded like a champagne bottle being uncorked startled Sandra. She couldn't imagine why Carlo would be serving champagne to a deliveryman, and then there was a loud crash that sounded like something hitting the floor. Sandra ran out into the hall and headed for his office. She stopped short as she heard Carlo and another man yelling in loud, angry voices. A chill ran down Sandra's spine and strange feelings erupted in the pit of her stomach.

"Get him out of here!" Carlo yelled. He was enraged and screaming obscenities.

"Whaddaya want me to do wid him?"

"You know what to do with him! Don't let anyone see you and keep your mouth shut. I'll clean up this mess."

Sandra quickly went back to her office. She didn't want to be seen but she wanted to hear what was being said. She was frightened. Of what she didn't know, but this didn't feel right. She pushed the door until it was almost closed, leaving it open just enough for her to see into the hall. Just then two men went by her office carrying a third man. He was hanging limp between the two of them; his eyes were closed and his face showed no sign of life. The delivery man had the limp man's feet, and another big hulk of a man, whom Sandra had never seen before, held him under the shoulders. When she looked at the limp man she shivered. Somehow she knew he was dead. They went out the door that led to the parking lot. She heard the sound of a car trunk being slammed shut and then a car's engine started.

Sandra was shaking. She couldn't believe what she had just heard. This man that she knew as such a kind, gentle man had just been screaming obscenities at someone in his office. And those men! They were carrying someone that looked like he was dead. That wasn't champagne popping. It must have been a gun, but guns are loud—it wasn't loud enough to be a gun, Sandra reasoned. She went to her desk and sat down. She needed to calm down. She wished she hadn't come back to the office, but she was here and she didn't know what to do now. Should she go to Carlo and ask what was going on or should she sneak out, go home and forget it? She was afraid to go outside in case those men were still there. She was afraid to confront Carlo about what she had just seen and heard. While she was sitting at her desk, Carlo Martini came barging into her office.

"What are you doing here?" he yelled at her, still enraged, red-faced and shaking.

Sandra shrunk back in her chair and stammered, "I, I forgot my checkbook. I came back for it. Are you all right? I heard loud voices, is there anything wrong?"

Carlo was beginning to get control. "It's all right, nothing's wrong, go home, Sandra. I'm just upset about something. It has nothing to do with you, it's nothing to concern you. Good night." He went back to his office and closed the door with a loud thud.

Sandra took some time to compose herself before she dared to venture into the dark parking lot to her car and drive herself home. She was upset over the events of the evening. It was bad enough leaving her checkbook at the office, but compared to the rest of the evening that was no big deal now. She kept going over what she had seen and heard. She couldn't get over the fact that Carlo had lost control. She had never heard him swear or yell at anyone. *Was that a gunshot I heard? Yes, it must have been. No, it couldn't be. Those two men carrying that guy, he looked like he was dead.*

Finally, at home, Sandra locked the door behind her and

made sure the shades were pulled down over the windows. A nice hot bath would help her relax and maybe take her mind off Carlo Martini and the events of the evening. As the hot water flowed into the bathtub, she poured her favorite bath oil into the water and lit a few candles. She was sure this would help her relax, and then she would have a glass of wine and settle down with that book she'd been reading. As she slipped out of her clothes and slid into the warm fragrance of the water she heard a loud cracking sound.

"Oh God, please help me. Let me relax, let me forget about what I saw tonight. Maybe I just thought I saw something bad, maybe it was nothing. Please, God, let it be nothing."

Sandra wanted to soak in the tub to relax her mind and body, but she couldn't relax no matter how good it felt. She felt vulnerable in the water with no clothes on. Images from old movies kept flashing through her head: women in tubs being drowned, stabbed… The house creaked again. Suddenly she could stand it no longer, and got out of the tub. Taking the towel, she half dried herself and slipped into her pajamas. Her terry bathrobe hung on the bathroom door. Grabbing it, she hurried barefoot to the kitchen where she poured herself a glass of wine. She curled up on the sofa with her book, but soon sleep overtook her. She spent a very restless night dreaming of men in shadows, Carlo Martini screaming at her, his face all distorted and her cowering in a corner. She woke several times, sobbing and soaked with perspiration. Saturday morning, Sandra woke feeling like she had a bad hangover. Her head hurt and her body was a mass of nerves.

"I need coffee, lots of strong coffee." Making her way to the kitchen, she made coffee. Then she opened the front door and picked up the newspaper from the front porch. She put the paper on the table. Coffee was what she needed. She couldn't care less about the state of the world. Right now the state of her world was totally confused.

The Hat Pin Murders

"Carlo! My job! Papa, why aren't you here? I need you! Dear God, what is going on? I am so scared and I don't know what to do about it. Help me, God. Help me to know what to do!" she screamed to the empty room, hoping God was listening.

Sandra sat curled up on the sofa drinking coffee. She had planned to sort through her father's things but she just wasn't up to it this morning, so she picked up the newspaper. There on the front page was a picture of the man that she had seen being carried out of the club last night. The headline read:

MOBSTER FOUND DEAD

> The body of mobster Joseph Bonillo was found last night in a dumpster behind the Church of the Good Shepherd in the downtown area. FBI agent Jim Reynolds, in charge of the investigation, said they are treating it as a mob execution. "Joseph Bonillo, Joey the Lip, was called that because of a scarred lip he got in a gang fight when he was a juvenile. We suspect his death is somehow related to his association with Carlo Martini. Martini has been in the rackets for years but we've never been able to get anything on him. He's been trying to get his business legitimate, but so far he has only accomplished that with his restaurants and nightclubs."

Sandra read the article again. She couldn't believe what she had read, but remembering the events of last night it all seemed to make sense.

"If it was anyone but Mr. Martini… He is such a nice man. I've known him for years. Papa worked for him for years, but Papa told me not to ask him any questions about his other businesses. Now I'm wondering why." Sandra needed to know what was going on and if the newspaper was right and Mr. Martini was a gangster and if that dead man was killed in his office, she certainly couldn't let Mr. Martini know what she had seen and heard. She was scared—if Mr. Martini was a gangster, she didn't want to work for him.

After thinking about it for a few minutes she decided to call the FBI's number that was listed in the paper. She dialed the number and was surprised when a man answered, saying, "FBI agent Jim Reynolds speaking."

"Hello, ah hello, I'm calling about the article in the newspaper. The guy that was killed, Joseph Bonillo. How do you know about these guys? Why do you think Carlo Martini is in the rackets? Is that like a gangster or a mafia person?"

"Who is this? Do you know something about this?"

"No," Sandra said, "I was just reading the paper. I was just wondering, that's all. I'm sorry to bother you."

"Lady, if you know something about this killing you could be in great danger. I can come to you. I can help you. If you have information it will be completely confidential."

"No, I really don't know anything, sorry." Sandra hung up the phone. Her heart was pounding and she was shaking all over. "Oh God, please help me! Papa, why did you have to die? I don't know what to do. I'm so scared." Sandra was exhausted. She sat at the kitchen table looking at the article for what seemed a very long time. She laid her head down on her folded arms and sobbed herself to sleep. A knock on the front door caused her to jump awake. She wasn't expecting anyone; it was Saturday morning and she was still in her pajamas and robe. Another knock and then the doorbell rang. She went to the door and jerked it open. She was in no mood for salesmen or company this morning.

A tall, handsome man wearing jeans, a casual shirt, and jacket was standing there. He was holding his hand up close to the screen door. She could see he was holding a kind of folded wallet with his picture on it.

"Agent Jim Reynolds, FBI. Miss Malone, may I come in? I think we need to talk."

The Hat Pin Murders

"How did you know where to find me? I didn't give you my name. And how do you know my name anyway?"

"We're the FBI, Miss Malone. I know you are a bookkeeper for Carlo Martini. Your father was his bookkeeper before you. I know your father passed away some time ago and you are his only child. I know everything about you, Miss Malone. What I don't know is whether or not you know anything about the murder of Joseph Bonillo. If you do, you are in real danger. Please, Miss Malone, let me come in. I can help you."

"Agent Reynolds, is that what you said?"

He nodded his head in the affirmative. "Yes, that's right, Agent Jim Reynolds."

"I've known Carlo Martini almost all my life and he is a very kind man. I have never seen anything that would lead me to think he is a killer and a mobster. I don't think we have anything to talk about. Please leave me alone."

"Miss Malone, you called my office after reading about the killing in the newspaper. That leads me to believe you know something. I'm sure you probably know nothing about the illegal things Carlo Martini is into."

Sandra started to cry. "I don't know what to do or who to trust. Okay, come in but let me see your identification again."

He pressed his identification against the screen. Sandra looked at it for a few seconds and then looked at his face. She reasoned that she wouldn't know a fake ID from a real one and the picture was definitely a picture of the man standing at her door.

If this is someone sent to kill me for what I saw last night they may as well get it over with right now, she thought. She unlocked the screen door and stepped back so he could enter.

They sat at Sandra's kitchen table and she told him everything she had seen at the club the night before. Sandra Malone had witnessed the murder of Joseph Bonillo. This was just what Agent Reynolds suspected. He needed to convince

Sandra to testify about what she had seen and heard. Then they could go over Carlo Martini's office with a fine-toothed comb and hopefully find something to match with Bonillo's DNA. It would be dangerous for Sandra, but Agent Reynolds assured her the FBI could protect her. On Monday morning at the time Sandra would report to work, the FBI was at the door of Martini's club with a search warrant. Their forensic people swept through the office and found Joey Bonillo's blood on the carpet and splatters on the front of Martini's desk. That was enough to link Carlo Martini and the two men that Sandra saw carrying Joseph Bonillo's body out of the club. Soon after, Carlo Martini was arrested and charged with the murder.

Sandra testified in court and Carlo Martini was found guilty and sentenced to twenty years in prison. His granddaughter Carla, a woman now, became enraged at the sentencing and threatened Sandra's life. Her brothers took her cursing and screaming from the courtroom.

* * *

Carlo Martini was a man with two different personalities: a loving and caring husband, father, and grandfather, and a ruthless gangster that had made his reputation early. His uncle, Salvatore Martini, had come from Sicily to the United States as a young man. He didn't have a nickel in his pocket when he arrived in Chicago, but he was strong, healthy, and determined. The streets of Chicago were not friendly to a young man, so Salvatore got by using his fists. It wasn't long before he had a gang of ruffians following him around. They collected money from every business on the street and in return protected them from the neighborhood gangs. Soon he was taking bets on sports events with a dozen or more young boys collecting the money for him. When a person placed a bet and lost, Salvatore was right there to collect the money. If the loser couldn't pay, Salvatore let his boys beat the fellow until he found a way to pay for his losses, or he would have to die. He was a force to be reckoned with, paving the way for the Martini family to be a leader in the Chicago world of crime. As the years went by, Salvatore became rich and powerful. The only thing he didn't have was a son to carry on his legacy. He did have a nephew, Carlo, who worshipped the ground he walked on.

By his sixteenth birthday Carlo had already killed a man in cold blood. It had to be done to protect the family; the family was everything. Carlo was smart and he was loyal. His uncle Salvatore saw great potential in him. Carlo would be the future of the Martini family.

"Carlo, you're a good boy and you're smart. I want you to stay close to me. I'll teach you everything. Some day you will run the family," Salvatore told him.

"Uncle Salvatore, you honor me. I'll stick close to you, do anything you want." From that day on, Carlo learned at the side of his uncle and mentor. When Salvatore became old and feeble he turned everything over to Carlo. Still, Carlo showed respect for his uncle by always asking his advice and getting permission before taking any action in a business deal. The family business grew and Carlo became very rich and powerful.

Chapter 15

She ran her hand over the lush purple fabric. Her fingertips caressed the soft, smooth material. Bringing it to her cheek, she closed her eyes and drank in its softness. A full bolt of the fabric was just waiting for her to claim it as her own. She unfurled its full length as she stood before a mirror; holding the soft, smooth fabric against her face. Perfect, yes, it was perfect. Her willpower left as the need for this elegantly expensive material claimed a place in her heart.

* * *

Marie Reader lived in a small house in a gated community in the little town of Sommer, Washington. She had come to Mercy Hospital with excellent recommendations and was hired to work in the accounting department of the hospital. Marie liked her coworkers but rarely socialized with them. She was known as a loner.

The women in the office where she worked had long ago quit asking her to go out for drinks after work or accompany them on weekend outings. Even several admiring doctors were turned away by her. She had no family and she was truly alone in the world. So she kept busy with her hobby of dressmaking. She was quite an accomplished seamstress, and designed and made all her own clothes. Jo-Ann Fabrics in nearby Spokane was her favorite place to shop for patterns, fabric, thread, and all the supplies she needed to sew her latest outfit.

Marie had not always been an expert seamstress. Immediately after moving to Sommer she had enrolled in classes at the local community college. She worked hard at fashion design and learning to make her own patterns. She even learned to transpose patterns that she had purchased into fashions unique only to her. When Marie couldn't find the fabric that was just right for the garment she wanted to make, the manager of the fabric store would place a special order for her. Marie found some beautiful purple wool and made herself a gorgeous suit and set it off with a silk blouse of a contrasting shade. She worked on the ensemble for weeks. Every detail was perfect, right down to the last button and stitch.

One Sunday as Marie was arriving home from church, her next-door neighbor Milly Good called to her. "Hi, Marie, did you just finish that suit? It's gorgeous!"

"Yes, I just finished the blouse yesterday, so I had to wear it to church this morning. I'm crazy about purple. I've noticed you wear a lot of purple, too."

"Of course I wear a lot of purple; I'm a Red Hat lady. We wear purple clothes and red hats. You need to come to lunch with me and my Red Hat friends sometime. You would love the girls. They're a great group. You'd fit right in."

Marie hesitated a moment, then said, "I don't know, Milly, I don't have much spare time. I'm just so busy."

"Nonsense," Milly said. "Next Saturday we're going to lunch and you're going with us. Wear this beautiful outfit. I want these gals to see what a real fashion plate looks like."

Marie went into her house. While she was undressing she began to think about what Milly had said. She had heard about the Red Hat Society. It sounded like a lot of fun and that was just what she needed, some fun. She knew Milly from church and the neighborhood, although they had never spent any time together. Marie felt Milly was someone she would enjoy spending time with. Yes, she would love to go out with Milly and her friends. She was ready for some girl talk and wished to spend some time with a group of fun-loving women. It had been a long time since she had done anything social. But what would she talk about? She didn't have a past, at least not one she wanted to share with strangers. The FBI had given her a past—a scenario that made sense to them—but it didn't make much sense to Marie.

Yes, I will go to lunch with Milly and her friends. I will just have to take control and if they start asking too many personal questions I will change the subject. After all is said and done it is my life and I don't have to talk about it if I don't want to. Then I will decide about any further lunches with Milly and her friends, she thought

All that week Marie was consumed with the thought of having lunch with Milly and her friends. Almost every day she made the decision to call Milly and tell her she was busy on Saturday and wouldn't be able to go to lunch. Each evening when she came home, Milly would be in her yard and give Marie a wave and a smile. Her kind, friendly neighbor boosted her confidence, and she would give in to the notion of joining her and her friends for lunch. Friday evening as Marie drove into her driveway and waited for the garage door to open, her next-door neighbor came running up to her.

"Marie, be ready tomorrow morning at eleven thirty. I'll drive. We're meeting the other girls at the Sommerset for lunch. It will be so much fun. Don't forget, we all wear purple, so you must wear that beautiful purple suit that you made. I bought a red hat for you. You're going to love it. I can hardly wait to see you in it. I'll see you at eleven thirty sharp!"

Wow, the Sommerset, I've wanted to see that hotel ever since I moved to this town. Milly bought me a red hat, so I certainly can't refuse to go. I'm going and I'm going to have fun. Marie's stomach began to churn—the thought of getting out socially caused her to let out a little giggle. "Yes, I am so excited about going to lunch with Milly and her friends."

The next morning Marie was up bright and early. She ate a light breakfast and tidied up around the kitchen, then went to her closet and took out her purple suit and the blouse she had finished making just one week ago. *It is beautiful,* she thought, *and I'm proud of my workmanship. All those classes at the college really paid off.* Marie put on her makeup and dressed. She fussed with her hair that was completely white.

So suddenly, yes, it turned white so suddenly. It was right after the trial, after being forced to move away from everything and everyone I knew and loved. Mamma never had white hair; it turned gray but never white. Forcing her mind back to the present, she wondered what the red hat was like. She couldn't ever remember wearing a hat before.

Mamma used to wear hats. They were always small and usually black. I always thought they were so old-fashioned looking. Oh, how I miss her. I wish I had one of those hats now. I lost almost everything. One suitcase with a few of Mamma's crocheted lace doilies and only one of Papa's sketches. It's not enough, it's not enough. Marie shook herself back to the present. She didn't need to dwell on the past, things she couldn't change.

"Maybe today will be the beginning of a new life, making new friends and wearing a hat for the first time. Who knows what the future will hold?"

At twenty-five minutes after eleven, the doorbell rang. Marie's heart began to race and she felt a little flustered. She opened the door to Milly standing there holding a beautiful, big-brimmed red hat with a huge red ribbon bow on the side. Milly smiled broadly as she held the hat out to Marie. Suddenly both ladies broke out in laughter.

"Here's your hat, honey, let's see how you look with it on." Milly put the hat on Marie's head and stood back to look. "Oh my, you look positively gorgeous!"

Milly looked pretty gorgeous herself. She was wearing a purple silk pantsuit with a purple feather boa hanging around her neck. Long, dangly earrings hung almost to her shoulders, and her red hair was pulled to one side. The hat she was wearing cupped her pretty face, showing off her green eyes.

"Milly, thank you so much. I must pay you for the hat. I do like it. I don't think I've ever worn a hat before." Marie giggled as she handled the brim of the hat.

"Glad you like it, honey, sometimes it takes a while to get used to wearing one. But you can't pay me for the hat. When you invite someone to join a Red Hat Club you give them a hat. So if you invite someone new then you will give them a hat, that's just the way it works. From now on, though, you have to buy your own. Come on, we don't want to be late."

On the drive to the hotel the two ladies chatted about the weather, the neighbors, and the flowers in their yards. It was nice, casual conversation and Marie felt very comfortable with Milly. When they arrived at the hotel's dining room, they were greeted by four other Red Hat ladies. They all introduced themselves to Marie. Jane, Martha, Sally, and Carrie all made her feel very welcome to the group. When they found out that Marie had made her outfit they were full of compliments. The main topic of conversation seemed to be clothes, hats, jewelry, hobbies, and where the next Red Hat gathering would be held.

"What is this Red Hat club all about and what do you do?" Marie asked.

"Oh, it's all about fun," Carrie said.

"Getting dressed up and spending time with friends," Martha added.

"I noticed how much attention we drew when we walked in. Is it always like that?" Marie asked.

"Yes, it's always like that," Sally said. "A lot of people think about their parents and grandparents sitting at home in their rocking chairs. When they see us all dressed up and having fun it gives them a new perspective on what senior citizens can do."

"Can you imagine anyone but a bunch of old ladies wearing purple and red together?" Martha asked.

"Speak for yourself," Milly said. "Hatties never get old;

we mature gracefully."

"Okay, okay, we can't expect Marie to join our group if we're fussing about such trivial things as age. Call the waiter—we need dessert!" Martha demanded.

"Yes, chocolate is what I need," Carrie said as she opened the dessert menu with a flourish.

"I'm gonna have this double chocolate brownie thing," Jane said.

"Do you want to share it?" Martha asked. "That thing is huge."

"Are you kidding? If I can't eat it all, I'll take it home," Jane said.

"It will still be good tomorrow."

"Chocolate every day, that's all I ask," Carrie said. "How about you, Marie, are you ordering dessert?"

"You make it sound irresistible; I'll have the chocolate cheesecake."

"See, girls, I told you she would fit right into our little group," Milly told them.

After a while they all said goodbye and they hoped Marie would join them at their next get-together.

"Milly, thanks for everything, I had such a good time," Marie said as they were leaving the restaurant. "All the girls are so much fun and I've always wanted to see the Sommerset Hotel. It is absolutely beautiful."

"I'm so glad you came with me. I knew you would fit right in with my zany friends. But Marie, I didn't ask about your age. You really are supposed to be fifty years old when you wear a red hat. If you're not fifty, I'll have to exchange the red hat for a pink one."

Marie started laughing. "I'll keep the red one. It took me a long time to get this white hair. It didn't come out of a bottle. I'm almost sixty if you must know."

"White hair is no indicator of age, these days. You have so

much energy I thought you might be younger," Milly told her.

"I've been thinking about retiring from the hospital after my next birthday and I've been worried about what I'm going to do with my days. I'd like to join you and your friends once in a while if that's all right."

"We'd love to have you, Marie. At the next gathering there will be several hundred Red Hat ladies attending. We put together a group we call The Singing Sisters and we will be performing. We sing the real old songs. We're not very good, but we love to sing. Some of the gals play the kazoo, that's the official instrument of the Red Hats."

"Sounds like you have lots of fun, Milly."

"Oh we do, and for our costumes we wear flapper dresses and cute little bands with feathery things on our head, like they wore in the roaring '20s. Come to our next practice, and if you want to join us, you can make your flapper dress with no problem."

"I love to sing. It sounds like fun. Let me know when you're meeting, I'd love to sit in with you." She was enjoying herself but suddenly wondered if she was jumping in too fast. "I don't want to get involved in too many things while I'm still working, Milly, but let me know the next time you get together and if I'm not busy I'll come."

On the drive home the two women talked and laughed. Marie was really enjoying herself. Milly pulled up in front of Marie's house and put the car in park.

"I'm so glad you came with me today," Milly said. "I've wanted to invite you for quite a while but you always seem to be in such a hurry. When I saw you in that purple suit on Sunday, I knew you were meant to be a Red Hat lady."

Marie got out of the car. "Milly, thanks again. I had a great time, and thank you for the hat, I love it. Bye now." Marie shut the car door and walked up to her house; she turned and waved to Milly. Inside the house, Marie looked at herself in the mirror that hung on the wall in her entry, and smiled at her reflection. She had had more fun today than she'd had in years. Those women were just having a little fun and enjoying life. Maybe she could have a normal life after all.

Friday evening Marie stopped at the grocery store on her way home from work and picked up a few things for the weekend. She had just put the bags of groceries on the kitchen counter when the doorbell rang. Marie knew it would have to be Milly. The gated community where she lived had a security guard on duty twenty-four hours a day. Only the residents had the combination to open the gate. Anyone else would be stopped and the guard would call the resident's home and notify them if they had a visitor. Marie never had visitors. Marie opened the door and there was Milly just as she suspected.

"Hi Marie," Milly said. "I just wanted to let you know the girls are coming over at seven tonight. We're gonna practice a few songs. Sorry for the late notice, but we just decided today."

"I just got home," Marie said. "I'll see how I feel at seven. If I'm not bushed I'll come by. Want me to bring anything?"

"No, we take turns with refreshments. Don't worry about that, just come at seven."

Marie shut the door. "Oh, wow! Sounds like fun, but right now I'm tired." She went to the bedroom and took off her clothes, hung them up, and got into her sweatpants and shirt.

Marie's bedroom was painted soft pastel pink, with lace curtains on the windows. The cream-colored chenille bedspread set off the four-poster bed and was similar to the one her mother bought for her when she was a young girl. When the FBI whisked her off to Sommer, she was only allowed to take a few items of clothing with her, and what she could fit into one suitcase. Nothing from her past that might be traced to her new identity. The FBI sold her father's home and all the furnishings. They set up the money in an account that no one could trace. Marie lived in an apartment for a number of years, calling little attention to herself. During that time she began her job at the hospital and took college classes in fashion design. She established herself in her job and the local church. She finally felt secure enough to purchase a home.

Marie picked up her mail from the gate guard, nothing but advertisements, a bill, and a fashion magazine. *Of course I don't get any real mail, who would I get mail from, anyway?* She started looking through the magazine, stopping on a page that showed a dress with a scoop neckline and a flowing skirt. "That would look great in purple with my red hat. Oh, listen to yourself, Marie: purple with red hats—you're really getting into it."

At ten minutes before seven the phone rang. Marie picked up the receiver and said, "Hello."

"It's Milly! You are coming over, aren't you?"

"I don't have to get dressed up, do I? I'm in my sweats and I really don't feel like changing."

"Come as you are, this is just a fun evening. We'll do a little singing and eating. Two of the girls are here already, you know them all. See you in a few minutes."

Marie hung up the phone. She was beginning to enjoy having friends once again. She slung her purse over her shoulder and went out the front door. As she started up the walk in front of Milly's house, a car pulled up and stopped. Two ladies got out of the car and both yelled a greeting to Marie. She waited for them, recognizing them from the luncheon last Saturday, but she had forgotten their names.

"Hi, Marie, isn't it? We were hoping you would join us tonight. I'm Jane and this is Martha. We're late because we stopped to pick up a pizza."

"It sure smells good. Glad to see you again," Marie said as they walked up to Milly's door and she rang the doorbell.

From inside someone yelled, "Come on in, it's open."

The three women walked into Milly's kitchen and they all started talking at the same time. Marie enjoyed the camaraderie and was starting to feel like she belonged. The pizza was placed on the kitchen table, and the girls helped themselves to sodas in the refrigerator and coffee that Milly had prepared. There was a bowl of fruit and a plate of cookies that everyone seemed to help themselves to.

"Dig in, Marie, help yourself to something to drink," Milly said.

"Let's finish up here. Then I want to know if you can carry a tune." Carrie licked some pizza sauce off her finger.

Marie took a piece of the pizza. It was good. She didn't care for soda, so she put some ice in a glass and filled it with water from the tap. "What kinds of songs do you sing? I used to do a lot of singing when I was a kid, and I sing in the choir at church. Yes, I can still carry a tune."

"Come in the living room so we can spread out, and let's give it a try. I've got the words to the song. Let's start with 'Bye Bye Blackbird.' Jane, you play the kazoo to keep us on tune."

Martha was holding the page with the words written on it. "This song is really old. I remember my mom singing it to me when I was little. Maybe that's the reason it's one of my favorites."

They all started singing together, then suddenly they all stopped except for Marie. She was a bit startled, but Milly motioned for her to continue.

"Marie, you sound terrific. You have a great voice. We have a lot of fun with our singing but none of us have a great voice like you. Please, please join us." Carrie got down on her knees and pressed her hands together, begging.

"Of course she will join us, she's having too much fun not to. We'll even let you sing a solo if you want. We're singing at the next Red Hat event. I've got the pattern for the flapper dress, but you have plenty of time to get it made," Milly said, smiling a big smile that told Marie how pleased she was to have her join the group.

Marie was very pleased, too. She really longed for the fellowship of these warm, friendly women. It had been a long time since Marie had let herself get involved with anyone, but she felt quite safe and secure with these new friends.

Marie took the pattern for the flapper dress home with her. Over the next several weeks she purchased the material and made her outfit that looked just like the others. "I'm finally getting to sing again," Marie said to her reflection in the full-length mirror. "I'm really enjoying being a part of the Singing Sisters. These women are just nice people. I feel safe with them." She practiced the songs and experimented with some dance steps. At their next rehearsal Marie suggested some dance moves they could do in kind of a chorus line. The women all loved it and practiced until they had it perfect. With Marie singing a solo and the new dance steps, they knew they would be a hit.

Finally the big day came. Marie was excited to be performing again. It was a Red Hat gathering and the Singing Sisters were the featured act. They sang two songs, Marie did her solo, and they did their dance routine. Marie was truly enjoying herself.

She hadn't been this happy since the last contest she had entered when her mother was still alive. A reporter from the local newspaper was there; she had been assigned to do an article on the Red Hats. Her editor had heard about the Red Hat phenomenon and wanted not only a story but pictures for the Sunday edition. When the Sunday paper came out, Marie's picture was right there on the front page.

"Oh my goodness," Marie said as she looked at herself. "Thank goodness Sommer is a small town with a small-town paper."

The doorbell rang and Milly yelled, "Hey, Miss Celebrity! Have you seen the morning paper?"

Marie opened the door and welcomed her neighbor and

good friend. "Come on in and let's have some coffee. I just can't believe they put me on the front page." Marie was obviously shaken.

"It was a great article and a good picture of you. I guess they took it when you were doing your solo. Anyway, they got you with your mouth closed and you're smiling, what more could you want?" Milly said as she poured herself a cup of coffee.

"I'd rather they put someone else in the paper. I'm not looking for any fame. I just want to live a nice, peaceful life and be left alone."

"It's a small town and a small-town paper. No one outside of Sommer will even see it. I can't see why you're so upset, it's not like they printed your address and phone number," Milly said as she settled at the kitchen table.

Marie was holding her coffee cup with both hands, taking warmth from the cup, hoping it would sooth her nerves. "Milly, you just don't understand. There are people that I don't want to know where I am. If they see my picture in the paper they will know I am here in Sommer. I can't talk about it, so please don't ask me any questions."

"I don't understand, but whatever the problem is you know I'm here for you. Come on, perk up. What's done is done. Let's enjoy the day." Milly reached across the table, took hold of Marie's hand, and gently squeezed it.

Chapter 16

Maggie invited everyone concerned to her house for coffee and dessert to celebrate the capture of Mary's murderer. Jessica made two of her famous apple pies and they were still warm when she arrived. Maggie had two ice cream makers full of homemade ice cream; one was vanilla and one was fresh peach. Ron Waters and his wife Nancy both came in carrying a plate of brownies. Frank had the coffee ready. He set out cream, sugar, and sweetener alongside the coffee mugs. Pitchers of ice water and iced tea were on the kitchen island beside the dessert plates, forks, and napkins.

Jessica busied herself dishing up the apple pies. Maggie had put Ellie and Becky Anderson in charge of the ice cream. Everyone seemed to want to taste everything. Plates were piled high with brownies, pie, and ice cream.

"Come on, help yourselves, there's plenty for everyone. After we eat we can let Ron fill us in. I know you're dying to know all the details. We can take our food outside on the patio. There's plenty of room for us all to sit out there," Maggie instructed her guests. Maggie was bustling around, talking and laughing. After months of emotional turmoil she could finally relax. The murderer was in jail. Could life finally get back to normal? She hoped so!

"Oh my, this pie is so good, and the homemade ice cream really tops it off," Ellie said between bites.

Jessica beamed at the compliment. "It's my pie, but Maggie made the ice cream and Nancy made the brownies. This is no time to be counting calories. It's time we did some celebrating. This whole affair must have been a terrible time for your family."

"It has been a very stressful time," Ellie told her. "Paul and Mary were very close and of course Becky was just crushed. Mary was so dear to all of us."

"These desserts are sure good, Maggie. Thanks so much for all you've done for us, the family really appreciates it. All the food you ladies brought out to the farm when the folks were here, it really helped. I don't think Ellie could have stood up under the strain if you hadn't come through like you did," Paul said as he sat his empty plate on the table beside his chair.

"It was the least we could do," Maggie said. "You know Mary was like a sister to me. Jessica and the other girls were very close to Mary, too. Our little Red Hat group won't be the same without her."

"That wasn't all these ladies did," Ron Waters said as he stood up, clearing his throat. "Maggie brought the killer down with a swing of her purse and a well placed karate chop.

Maggie interrupted. "I hope you all know Kate Bennett and her brother John. Kate is the real hero. She actually saw Carla murder Mary, although she didn't know it at the time. Then at the fashion show she spotted her again and Carla tried to kill poor Marie Reader. If Phil, the mall manager, hadn't gone back there and stopped her, she probably would have succeeded. Marie has been a long time recovering, but thank God she's on the mend."

Jessica spoke up. "Then she tried to kill Maggie and me by ramming the back of Frank's Mustang! Let me tell you I was pretty scared. Maggie outran her; she punched that little car and did some fancy driving and lost her. We thought Frank would kill us for wrecking his car, but he was pretty good about it."

"Yeah"—Frank laughed and slapped the arm of his chair—"that little car can get up and go, and it is my pride and joy! But, Maggie and Jess are a little more important than a car, I guess. After killing Mary and wounding Marie and Phil at the mall, that Carla Martini was pretty desperate, I'd say."

Kate spoke up. "She tried to kill me, too, or at least I think that was on her mind at the time. She pushed me hard and that bump on my head ended up a concussion. And those two boys! I think those kids had the adventure of their lives."

"Yes, she was really on a rampage," Ron Waters said. "You're all very lucky. She is a violent and ruthless killer."

Paul asked, "Who is this Carla Martini, anyway?"

"Carla Martini is the granddaughter of Carlo Martini. He was head of one of the biggest crime families in Chicago," Ron told them. "She was obsessed with her grandfather and wanted to take his place as head of the family some day."

"But Ron, what I want to know is why? Why in the world did she kill Mary and then try to kill Marie?" Milly Good asked.

"Killing Mary was a mistake! Marie Reader—or should I say Sandra Malone—was her real target," Ron said as he got up and paced around the patio. "I talked to the FBI guys. They're usually very tightlipped about these things, but since you all were so involved in her capture, I got an okay to fill you in. Sandra Malone, you know her as Marie Reader. She was a bookkeeper for Carlo Martini. Anyway, she witnessed a murder and knew that Martini was involved. She got scared and called the FBI. She testified against Martini and he was sent to prison for twenty years, where he died. Carla threatened Sandra's life, so the FBI had her placed in the witness protection program and she was relocated to Sommer. Everything was fine until some reporter took her picture and put it in the local newspaper. Since this Red Hat thing has gone so crazy, the press is picking up any story they can find. Her picture and the story were picked up by the national press. Martini's granddaughter, Carla, recognized Marie's picture. So she came after her."

"So she got a job at the Sommerset? But they called her Ann. Did she get hired there under a false name?" Maggie asked.

"Ann is her middle name, and she simply told them that

she preferred going by Ann. It was just a matter of a nametag. She knew the Red Hats were meeting at the Sommerset and she just waited." Ron was about to continue.

"Why did she kill Mary if she was after Marie?" Paul wanted to know.

"The Singing Sisters didn't sing at that event. Apparently she just kept watching and asked around. She asked about Marie Reader and apparently someone pointed out Mary Reed. The names were close enough and they looked a little alike."

Kate spoke up. "I told you, Maggie. Your friend Mary kept saying, 'I don't know what you're talking about—that's not who I am.' Remember, Maggie, remember I told you that?"

"Yes, Kate, I remember you telling me that. You didn't realize it but you saw Mary being murdered."

"I'm glad I didn't know what was happening," Kate said. "I would have been so scared!" Kate shivered at the thought. Maggie took her hand and gave it a reassuring squeeze.

"It's a good thing she didn't know you were watching her, she would have gone after you, too."

"I was very careful, lieutenant. I knew she was up to no good, but I sure didn't know it was murder."

Ron continued. "Carla read the obituary and that was when she realized she had killed the wrong person. Then Maggie and Jessica started asking questions and she wasn't ready to leave town. That was when she tried to run you off the road. You were very lucky. She would probably have killed you both if you hadn't outrun her. Remember she had a gun."

"So that was her in that black Mercedes. The windows were all blacked out so we couldn't see her. She's really insane," Jessica said.

"When she heard the Red Hats were doing a fashion show at the mall, she went there and waited. After Marie sang, Carla followed her behind the stage. She attacked Marie and cut her up pretty bad." Ron shook his head and went on. "That was when Phil Wallace, the mall manager, fell over Marie and probably saved her life. Carla was bending over her and Phil fell right into her. Phil yelled and tried to fight her off, then Carla ran off. Phil started after her, and she shot him."

Kate jumped up. "That's when she tried to get past me, but I stopped her. She pushed me down and threatened me with that gun. She said, 'Are you stupid or something?' I guess I was, but all I wanted to do was to stop her from getting away. Johnny helped me up and he was a little upset with me. The paramedics checked me over and thought all I had was a big bruise on my arm but later we found out I had a concussion."

"That's right, Kate, you slowed her down with your defensive move, then Maggie hit her with her purse and karate chopped her." John threw his head back, laughing.

"I'd give anything to have seen that. Then I guess it was you, John, who taped her hands and ankles? She was tied up like a Christmas package when I arrived on the scene," Ron said with a chuckle.

"Oh my goodness, I feel so bad now," Milly said, shaking her head. "You know Marie lived next door to me. She was so quiet and didn't seem to have any friends or family. She really enjoyed herself every time we got together with the Red Hats. She seemed to be starved for friendship. I was so excited about that article in the paper. I didn't understand why she was so upset about the picture. Now I understand and I just feel terrible."

"It's no one's fault." Ron tried to reassure her. "That's the chance you take when you go into the witness protection program. There's always the possibility someone will recognize you. She could have contacted the authorities and had them move her again. That would have involved a whole new identity and starting all over again. It's very complicated and very difficult and maybe she just didn't want to go through it again. Now that Carla is in custody I'm pretty sure Marie will be able to live a normal life once she recovers from her injuries."

"So what's going to happen to this Carla now?" Paul asked. "I hope they put her away for a long time."

"With all the witnesses against her, there's a good chance for conviction," Ron said. "The FBI has taken over the case because it involves the Chicago mob. I understand she's doing a lot of talking, hoping to make some kind of deal."

"Do you mean she could get off?" Paul demanded.

"No, there's no chance of her getting off. After all, she killed Mary—premeditated murder. Then there was the attempt on Marie and Phil and assault on Maggie and Jessica and on Kate. No, I can't see her getting off; she just wants to avoid the death penalty. Some of you may be called to testify. I hope that answers most of your questions. We will just have to wait for the trial now."

"At least we know what happened. Thank you, all of you. You've been good friends," Paul said.

Becky got up and walked over to Maggie. "I want you to know that I'm so sorry, I've been kind of a brat. Since Aunt Mary died, I've been doing a lot of soul searching. She wanted me to go to college and that's what I'm going to do. I haven't figured out what I want to do with my life, but I enrolled last week and I'll start classes when the new term starts. I want to make Aunt Mary proud of me."

Maggie got up and hugged Becky. "I'm so happy. That's exactly what Mary wanted. She loved you so much. I know you'll make her very proud."

* * *

Things were getting back to normal at the Coppenger house. Maggie felt she could move on with her life now that Mary's murderer had been arrested. She still missed her dear friend but the pain of her loss was getting easier to bear as each day passed.

Frank had taken his Mustang for repairs to a garage that specialized in classic cars. "The damage was minimal because a classic Mustang is made of metal, so it's a pretty solid car, not plastic like the new ones. Some bodywork and a new paint job and she'll be as good as new. But you might think about using something else for the parade next year," Frank told Maggie.

* * *

When Darlene found out who her friend Ann really was and about the murders she committed, Darlene went to Maggie and apologized. "I'm so sorry for those awful things I said to you about Mary. I thought Ann was my friend. To think she used me to get to Marie, and she almost killed her, and she did kill Mary. Now that I think of it she might have killed me if I had crossed her. I couldn't believe what everyone said about her so I went to the jail to visit her. She was so mean and hateful to me. That's when I realized she had used me."

Maggie hugged Darlene. "I'm just glad it's over and she didn't kill anyone else. You know she tried to run Jessica and me off the road that day we were at the hotel asking her questions. Ron said she would probably have killed us if we hadn't outrun her."

"I am so sorry, Maggie, please forgive me."

"It's over, Darlene, we have to move on. All is forgiven." Maggie gave Darlene a reassuring smile.

"I saw the Mustang, that beautiful car, all crunched in the back. I'll bet Frank was really mad."

"Well, the car's fixed and it's as good as new. Now, what about you?" Maggie asked.

"Becky and I both signed up for college classes. Neither one of us know what we want to be. I think Becky is leaning toward teaching. We've got to get our general classes in first."

"I'm sure your father would be pleased that you're going to college."

The Hat Pin Murders

"Daddy left me a trust fund and Mary left the house and some money to Becky, so we're both in good shape financially. You know, after this deal with Ann I've found out that Becky is a pretty good friend to have. She's just plain ol' Becky. I know I can trust her."

Maggie was pleased at what she was hearing. "I think you both are pretty special. I hope you will come by once in a while and let me know how you are doing."

"I'll do that. I'm going by Becky's now. See you later," Darlene said as she went out the door and got in her little sports car that was parked in front of Maggie's house.

* * *

The Mystery Mamas hold their regular monthly meeting at Marie Calendars, on the second Thursday of the month, at eleven thirty in the morning. They have a standing reservation and the restaurant always has their table ready with twelve places set. The Hatties try to arrive at the same time and together they parade through the dining area, usually receiving a round of applause from the other customers.

When the Red Hats meet it is a fun time of getting together for a good visit and of course a chance to dress in their finest regalia, making sure they are noticed by everyone.

This is the fun part of the Red Hatting. Putting on a bright purple outfit, all the jewelry and feathers you can find, and of course an elegant red hat to top it off.

The October meeting was a sad occasion because of Mary's empty chair. The girls took turns sharing some happy story they remembered about their dear friend. They ended the lunch by everyone ordering huckleberry cheesecake, Mary's favorite dessert.

The November lunch was a time to give thanks. Maggie stood. Using her knife, she tapped her glass that held raspberry iced tea. After she had everyone's attention she raised her glass. "Hatties, we have a lot to be thankful for. Mary's killer is in jail."

They all gave a toot on their kazoos.

"Frank's Mustang looks like new again, Jess and I survived without whiplash, and soon Mary's empty seat will be filled again."

Another toot.

They all drank a toast, and then with their kazoos played a rousing chorus of "We are the Red Hat Girls."

Maggie was facing the entrance and just as they all sat down she saw John Bennett and Kate enter the restaurant. John spoke to the hostess, who pointed him to where the Red Hats were seated.

"Look, Johnny, there's Maggie and her friends," Kate said, pointing toward the Hatties' table.

Maggie got up and greeted them. "Kate, we would like you to have lunch with us. I'll take you home later."

Kate had a look of confusion on her face. "But, Johnny said he was taking a few hours off work to take me to lunch for a little celebration."

"Yes, I did take off a few hours, but not to have lunch with you. I was supposed to bring you here to have lunch with Maggie and the Red Hat ladies. They want you to join their group. Maggie will bring you home later and you can tell me all about it this evening. I have to get back to work now. So have fun, bye." John turned to Maggie. "Thanks, Maggie, thanks a lot."

Kate gave John a little tap on his arm with her fist. "John, you brat, you didn't tell me...."

"It wouldn't have been a surprise if I'd told you. So have fun and I'll see you later," John said as he turned and walked away.

Maggie took Kate's hand and led her to the empty chair.

"You will sit here. This is where Mary used to sit, and we want you to take her place in our group."

"Oh wow! I'll be a part of a Red Hat group. Thank you all, this is so neat," Kate said. "And such a surprise!"

Rita stood up, pushed her chair back, and placed a hatbox on the chair. "Kate, only women that are fifty years old can wear a red hat. We know that you are not fifty."

Kate's happy smile suddenly turned to a frown. "Oh, I'm sorry, but I thought you said you wanted me to be a part of your Red Hat group."

Rita opened the hatbox and took out a beautiful pink hat with a big pink silk rose on it. "Kate, we want you to join our group. You are our new little sister, and little sisters wear pink hats." Rita placed the pink hat on Kate's head and all the Hatties stood and clapped their purple and red-gloved hands.

Chapter 17

Maggie and Frank sat at their kitchen table. Frank was reading the paper while he sipped his second cup of morning coffee. Maggie held her cup with both hands. Feeling the warmth of the coffee through the porcelain cup always gave her the feeling of security. She surveyed her beautiful kitchen. After twenty years in this home they had finally done some remodeling. Her kitchen was perfect now, real hardwood floors, granite countertops, and brand new stainless steel appliances. Maggie's favorite was the new stainless steel sink and faucet with the pull-out spray! Of course she had a new automatic dishwasher but Maggie loved to stand at the sink full of warm, soapy water and wash the dishes herself. This was a time that she enjoyed just looking out at the woods beyond their backyard. She would search the area for deer that sometimes came down looking for new grazing spots. Once they even had a family of moose that camped out in their yard. Neighbors came from all around to take pictures. After three days the excitement wore thin and animal control was called. The moose were tranquilized and taken to Turnbull Refuge just outside Cheney, Washington. Maggie had everything she could possibly want as far as material things were concerned. Everything should be wonderful now but Maggie still had a hollow feeling inside her.

"Maggie, are you okay? You seem so far away." Frank folded his paper and laid it on the table.

"I just lost my best friend! She was senselessly murdered and I found her, it was just awful. It still hurts like it was just yesterday. I don't think I'll ever get over it."

"I know, sweetheart, I wish there was something I could

do to make this all go away." Frank looked at his wife of almost forty years—he loved this woman with all his heart and it pained him to see her suffer so.

"I was thinking about Carla Martini." Maggie's hands clutched the cup so hard she spilled the coffee. "She's so young and so full of hate and anger. I can't imagine that she ever had a friend." Maggie continued as she mopped up the coffee with her napkin. "What would make someone so young commit such a hideous murder?"

"I don't know, Maggie." Frank lowered his head and stared at his cup. "I can't imagine murdering another human being."

"It seems if she hadn't been stopped she wouldn't think twice about killing anyone else if they got in her way." Maggie looked out the window. "I just can't understand that kind of hate."

"She's out for number one, that's for sure. It just makes you wonder what kind of childhood she had. Her grandfather was the head of a real mafia crime family."

"I thought the mafia was all done away with," Maggie said. "Al Capone and that Teflon character, John Gotti. I thought he was the last when they put him away."

"They are all about money and power. It's hard to let go of the kind of power those people have. When one of the big guys is put in prison or killed, one of the little guys makes his move to take over." Frank shook his head. "They're all just waiting for their turn to be the one that calls the shots, gives the orders."

"Greed! I guess Carla was greedy for power, too. Ron said she was obsessed with her grandfather. She wanted to be just like him." Maggie looked at Frank with tears welling up in her eyes. "Do you suppose she really loved him, or was it the evil power she loved?"

"Power means money. People will do most anything for money."

"She is so full of hate!" Maggie shook her head.

"You see how it can get hold of you. You are pretty near hating Carla. Don't let it consume you, Maggie. She will get what's coming to her. Ron said she's spilling her guts to the FBI, hoping to get a reduced sentence."

"Reduced sentence? What do you mean by that?" Maggie asked.

"Seems that she's telling everything she knows about anybody that might be of interest." Frank gave a little snort and shook his head. "She's talking about guys she remembers from her childhood."

"She couldn't get away with it, could she? When we all testify they won't be able to ignore all the evidence against her, will they?"

"Ron doesn't think you will have to testify, Maggie. It looks like she's pleading guilty."

"Would they do that? Give her a reduced sentence? She killed Mary, and what is it they say on TV—conspiracy to commit murder? She tried to kill Phil and Marie and assaulted Kate and how about me and Jess getting rammed in your car? Poor Marie, I'd be surprised if she doesn't have nightmares for the rest of her life."

"Maggie, can you imagine what would happen to Kate if some attorney got her on the witness stand? She's just a kid, and I think she is still pretty vulnerable from her parents' death. Those attorneys can be ruthless. They would tear her to shreds on the witness stand. Who knows what they would bring up? They could bring up the fact that she has had some emotional problems in the past and that could be pretty devastating for her."

"Oh, Frank, I've been so obsessed with wanting that Carla to get what's coming to her I hadn't thought about what it would be like for Kate to testify in court."

"Well, even for you it wouldn't be pleasant," Frank told

her. "The way you hit Carla with your purse and that karate chop, they would probably make you out to be the bad guy and Carla to be the victim."

"Yes, you're probably right," Maggie agreed. "And Marie, we can only imagine what she's already been through."

"Her testimony put Carla's grandfather away. She had to give up her whole life and start over again, new name and all. I can't imagine going through that."

"Oh my, Marie would probably have to testify. After all she is the one Carla was after." Maggie suddenly realized how deeply Marie was involved in this whole affair.

"That poor woman, can you imagine how deep the scars run, both physical and emotional? All I've been thinking about was Mary and how much we all love and miss her. Poor Marie has no one and it was her that Carla meant to kill. I can't imagine how lonely and frightened she must be."

"Marie could really use a friend." Frank smiled at Maggie, knowing that she would do the right thing.

"There's so much to consider. Milly said Marie has no family and it took a long time for her to make friends. Oh, Frank, I've been so wrapped up in myself I haven't been to visit her."

"You can only do what you can do."

"Marie's a Red Hat lady and that makes her a sister. I'll call Milly and get her phone number. Maybe Kate and I will give her a visit."

"Kate certainly knows how to cheer people up. She might be good for Marie," Frank acknowledged.

"I'm going to try my best to leave well enough alone and try to put this whole Carla thing behind us. I'm glad you always keep a cool head about you, Frank." Maggie reached over and squeezed her husband's hand.

"My cool head is telling me I need to get some things done in the yard before the freezing weather comes." Frank got up and pushed his chair up to the table. "Have you girls decided where you're holding your Christmas lunch?"

"Rita's taking care of making the reservations. I really don't care as long as it's not at the Sommerset Hotel. It's going to take a while before I'm ready to go back there. Anyway, we're supposed to make something for our exchange gift. I'm making one of my pincushion dolls. We're not supposed to spend a lot of money. It's just for fun."

"Good, that means more for you to spend on me," Frank said as he winked at Maggie. "No wonder some of you gals have Red Hat rooms. You keep accumulating stuff."

"Well, I've got to get in gear. I'm picking Kate up at ten. We're going to the craft store. She said she knows what she wants to make for her gift. She's one talented young lady."

"I sure like her and her brother, John. They are good people," Frank told her.

"She fits right in with our little group. She is just a joy to be around. And she's added some spark to our gatherings. Some of the older ladies seemed to have perked up since Kate joined us."

"I agree, she is a sweetheart. But I've got to get out of here and get some work done. Tell Kate hello for me and you two have fun."

Maggie cleaned up the kitchen, then went to the bedroom where she made the bed.

She loved the sturdy four-poster bed and especially the soft peach canopy that covered the top with its lace and fringe. The bed skirt was soft and flowing with a matching comforter over the top. Seven pillows were piled high against the headboard. Frank was such a good sport about all the frills and lace. He would laugh and say that it reminded him of one of those naughty ladies brothels on those old westerns that he loved to watch on TV. Then he would snuggle up to Maggie and tell her it was the most exciting room in the house. Maggie laughed as she remembered the last time he said that.

Maggie went to the closet to choose something to wear. She dressed in blue jeans and a knit top, then put on her walking shoes, hoping she could keep up with Kate. After fixing her hair and face she went to the phone and dialed Kate's number. "Hi, Kate, it's Maggie, are you ready to do some serious shopping?"

If Maggie could have had a daughter of her own, she hoped she would be just like Kate. Kate was beautiful—not in the Hollywood kind of beauty, but the inner beauty that shines through. She was innocent and caring and full of excitement about everything and everyone that she encountered. What a joy to be around someone so full of life. Maggie was grateful to have Kate and John in her life.

Chapter 18

Maggie woke early Christmas Eve morning. Basking in the glorious wonders of the season, she turned her thoughts toward heaven. She had been dreaming when she woke. All her confusion was gone and the perfect peace of God filled her heart and mind.

"Joy to the world, the Lord is come! Let earth receive her king. Let every heart prepare him room." Maggie's voice was sweet and clear as she sang the words to one of her favorite Christmas carols.

Frank came into the kitchen and joined Maggie in a duet, blending their voices in praise to the Lord.

"And heav'n and nature sing, and heav'n and nature sing, and heav'n and heav'n and nature sing."

Maggie turned to embrace her husband. As he pulled her to him their lips met in a soft kiss.

"Merry Christmas, Frank, isn't Christmas just glorious?"

"Yes, all the hope for the world is wrapped up in Christmas. When Jesus came to earth He gave us a new beginning. He came as a tiny baby, then died on the cross, taking our sins with him. When he arose from the grave he conquered everything that was mean and evil. It's hard to understand but I'm sure He is working even through all the tragic events of these past months."

"He is, and it's the best Christmas present I could ever have wished for. The new year will be bright with promise and new hope. Frank, I had a dream last night, and when I woke up this morning everything was crystal clear."

"What do you mean everything was crystal clear?"

The Hat Pin Murders

"You know these past months since Mary's death I've been so angry."

Sitting at the kitchen table, their coffee cups filled with the fresh hot brew they both savored, Frank waited for his wife of forty years to continue. She needed release from the anguish that had been pent up all these months. Watching her face, he knew she was struggling to find the words she needed to express what was in her heart.

"Anger is part of the grieving process," Frank said. "The way Mary died was enough to make even a stranger angry. She was your best friend, like a sister to you. It takes time, Maggie; don't be so hard on yourself. Now, what's this about a dream?"

"I had a dream last night and I believe it is God's Christmas gift to me. In my dream I saw Mary coming towards me. She was a long way off and I could see that she was running and skipping as she came toward me. She was waving and smiling and she shouted something to me. I couldn't make out what she was saying. But finally she ran right up to me. She was so beautiful and so happy and looked so young. I've never seen her happier. Her eyes were sparkling and she was laughing. It was so real. I think it was real, Frank."

Maggie paused and looked out the window, her eyes filled with tears. Looking back at her husband she said, "Frank, I think God allowed Mary to come to me in my dream so I would know that she is all right."

"That's beautiful, Maggie," Frank said as he looked into her eyes.

"But that's not all; she spoke to me." Maggie closed her eyes and wiped her tears with the sleeve of her robe. Looking back at Frank her expression changed. She smiled a very contented smile. "Mary took my hands and looked right into my eyes. She just seemed so happy, and then she spoke. 'Oh, Maggie! Hank was there to meet me. He was waiting for me and he took me in his arms and I felt so safe and happy. I'm happy, Maggie, don't worry about me. Hank is here with me. Forgive, Maggie, you must forgive.' Then I woke up and had this wonderful peace. I'm sure God gave me this dream to tell me she was all right; she's in heaven with Hank. Isn't that just the best Christmas gift ever?"

"Yes, it sure is. You know Mary was never really happy after Hank died. She was just going through the motions. We miss her here but heaven is a much happier place with her there, I'm sure."

"She told me to forgive, Frank, Mary said forgive. I have to forgive Carla. That's the hard part, but I think I can now. I really think I can forgive her."

Maggie rose from the table; she gathered their dirty breakfast dishes, rinsed them, and placed them in the dishwasher. "I need to get busy. John is bringing Kate over. What are you boys going to do today?"

"Oh, I'm sure we'll think of something."

"Kate's helping me get things ready for tomorrow's dinner."

"What are we having, Christmas goose?"

Maggie flicked Frank with the kitchen towel she was holding. "No, we're not having Christmas goose! We're having a Christmas ham! But we won't worry about that until tomorrow morning. Kate's helping me with the side dishes and a centerpiece for the table. Maybe we can finish decorating the tree."

The doorbell rang. Frank opened the door to see Kate's beautiful smiling face before him. She barged through the door carrying a large plastic tote.

"Merry Christmas, Frank! Where's Maggie? I brought stuff to decorate. Johnny's waiting for you in the car. Don't come back until you have bags full of Christmas presents!"

"Merry Christmas to you. Maggie's in the kitchen. You two have fun. We'll see what we can do about those presents."

Frank paused before going out the door to marvel at the energy that seemed to explode out of this pretty young girl.

Kate placed her tote on a chair and began unbuttoning her coat. "Maggie, I'm here. What are we going to do? We need to decorate the tree and fix a nice centerpiece for the dining room table. Can I help with the food? I'm so excited I can hardly stand it."

"Kate, come over here and sit down. I know it's Christmas and I'm always excited about Christmas but you act as if you might blow a gasket. Come and sit down. Have you had breakfast?"

"Oh yes, I ate breakfast a long time ago. It feels like it might be time for lunch though."

"Here you go, Frank and I had muffins and fruit just a little while ago. Dig in and tell me why you're so excited."

"Well, this is the first time since our parents died that Johnny and I have spent Christmas with a family. We always go to church either Christmas Eve or Christmas morning. Then we go out to a nice restaurant for Christmas dinner. Then we go home and exchange presents. It's always really nice and Johnny always tries to make it special for me. But it's not like having a family."

"Oh, you poor dear, I had no idea. You and Johnny are part of a family now! From now on Christmas will be a family affair with decorations, dinner with all the trimmings, and presents and singing and anything else you want to do."

"Frank and Johnny went shopping; what do you think they will get for us? Johnny always gets me something to wear and then he thinks up some crazy fun stuff, too."

"Go ahead, have another muffin. I've wanted to ask you about your parents but I didn't want to push you or seem nosy. Do you mind talking about it?"

"Oh no, I don't mind. I don't like to talk about it when the person asking is just being nosy, but it's okay, I don't mind telling you." Kate paused to take a bite of her muffin and a swallow of milk. "I was a freshman in high school. The school year had just started. My dad had to go on this business trip and Mom wanted to go with him. They hadn't gone away by themselves in years. Mom said she just wanted a little holiday. I wanted to go with them but since school had just started they said I needed to stay home. Johnny would be there and I was old enough to get myself off to school in the mornings. After all it would only be for a few days. I acted like a real brat and said something mean. I forget what I said but I remember Mom's eyes filling with tears and I refused to kiss her good-bye." Kate took a napkin from the holder in the middle of the table and blotted her eyes before she continued. "They were killed in a car crash on their way home. That was the last time I ever saw them."

"Oh honey, I'm so sorry. It must have been terrible for you. So you and John have been taking care of each other since then."

"I felt so guilty about the way I talked to Mom that day. I couldn't stand myself. I blamed myself for everything. Anyway, the day of the funeral I got so upset I had a seizure. They put me in the hospital and said it was caused from stress and guilt. I spent months in what Johnny called a special school but really it was a hospital. I got lots of good counseling and was able to go back to my old high school the next year. But I was a freshman again, a whole year behind all my friends. It wasn't so bad, but Johnny has been so protective of me. He thinks any little thing will send me over the edge again."

"Johnny loves you very much, Kate. You are all he has."

"I know. I just wish he would loosen up a little. He thinks I'll have another seizure. I don't blame myself anymore. I know I was a teenage brat and the accident wasn't my fault. I had a nervous breakdown and Johnny thinks it might happen again if I get too stressed out. Johnny worries so much, but he's a wonderful brother."

"I think you're both pretty wonderful. I'm just glad things worked out the way they have, bringing us together. Now let's get busy on our Christmas projects."

"Maggie, I imagine you think it's pretty weird, me going to that Red Hat event at the Sommerset. Just a kid, wearing a red hat and all, but if I hadn't been there I wouldn't have seen the murder. You see, my mom read this article in the newspaper about the Red Hats. She thought it sounded like a lot of fun and was planning to join a group after their trip. She bought the hat and sweater that I wore that day."

Maggie listened intently to Kate's words. *Dear God, this poor child has been through more than most adults*, Maggie thought.

"Anyway," Kate continued, "I guess I was trying to make a connection to Mom somehow. You know, going there to see what it was all about. I asked Johnny to take me to lunch at the Sommerset." Kate gave a little laugh. "Johnny will do anything for me. You know, trying to keep me from getting all stressed out. Anyway, I got all dressed up and put on the red hat. After lunch I told him I wanted to see what those Red Hat ladies were doing in the ballroom. He said he would wait in the bar because they had a game on the big-screen TV and I could take my time. I tried to talk to some of the ladies but I guess they saw I was just a kid and thought I was up to no good. I was going to get Johnny to go home when I saw that Carla take the doll into the ladies' room. I thought that was kinda funny so I watched her and that was when she started talking to your friend Mary. That was when I saw her yell at Mary and when she hit her, I got scared and found Johnny and told him I wanted to go home."

"Oh, Kate, you poor dear. You've been through so much. Thank you for sharing that with me. I hope from now on all our lives are going to get back to normal. Speaking of normal, I'm glad we went to visit Marie."

"Yeah, me too, I can't imagine what she's been through. I had heard of the witness protection program but I thought it was just something they told about in the movies. I can't imagine leaving everything and everyone and going to a totally new place to live. At least I have Johnny and you have Frank; poor Marie didn't have anyone. Maybe we could do something nice for Marie for Christmas, what do you think?"

"Good idea, Kate, you are always so thoughtful. But we have Christmas to get ready, young lady." Maggie gave Kate a little hug. "Christmas waits for no one!"

Kate picked up her tote and brought it to the dining room table. Inside she had tree ornaments, ribbon, and several angel figurines. Maggie had purchased a beautiful poinsettia plant and at least a dozen candles. Kate took inventory and began to assemble the centerpiece. She placed the angels in the center of the table and arranged the ornaments and candles around them. She was making bows with the ribbon when Maggie came to see what she was doing.

"Kate, this is lovely!"

"I'm going to hang a big bow on each side of the window, if that's okay with you. I think it will be very festive."

"We can light the candles when we sit down to eat. You never cease to amaze me with your artistic talents."

"Let's put the poinsettia on the entry table. Frank put some fresh pine branches on the front porch. I want to bring some inside and place them around the plant."

"Beautiful! It's perfect, the aroma of fresh pine—"

"We'll light the tree and sing songs," Kate interrupted. "We'll eat and eat and then we'll open presents!"

"Merry Christmas, Kate," Maggie told her.

"And God bless us every one!" they both said in unison.

Chapter 19

Marie Reader couldn't understand why her life had been spared. She would be better off if it had ended that day in the mall; each day since had been a struggle. If it hadn't been for her neighbor, Milly Good, banging on her door every morning, Marie would have spent the day in bed.

Milly made it her business to get Marie out of bed each morning. "Get dressed, put on your makeup, fix your hair, eat! If I have to dress you and feed you, I will!"

The doctor said Marie was making good progress. The scar along her neck and shoulder was deep. The physical therapy helped her to get some strength in her arm. But Marie really didn't care if she got better or not. She regretted her life, the decisions she had made. Her father had encouraged her to marry Jason. He didn't want her to be alone after he was gone. Marie was determined to take care of her father; she cared about nothing else.

I was so stupid, I could have had Jason and maybe a family and could have taken care of Papa, too. Now I have nothing. Jason would have stood beside me through all those years, he would have protected me. Now I have nothing to live for.

Day after day Marie slid deeper and deeper into a dark hole of depression. Milly tried her best to help her friend until she was ready to give up on her. As a last resort Milly called on friends in her Bible study group and some of the Red Hat ladies.

"I'm worried about Marie; I think she's close to being suicidal. I'm asking you all to join me in prayer. If we bombard heaven on her behalf maybe she will escape this awful depression and come back to being her old beautiful self again."

The ladies prayed feverishly for an hour. Finally as if a heavy weight had been lifted they each began to praise God.

"Suddenly I feel happy," Milly said.

"Yes," Jessica said. "I think God heard our prayer."

"This doesn't mean we can stop praying for Marie. She still needs a lot of healing, body and mind. I think I'll go next door and see how she's doing. You gals go ahead and eat. I'll take one of these sandwiches to her. Maybe I can get her to eat something. When you're through here you can let yourself out. See you all later."

Milly put a sandwich on a small plate, covered it with plastic wrap, and carried it to Marie's house next door. She let herself in and called out, "Marie, it's me." Surprised to see Marie standing in the kitchen, Milly said, "Marie, you're up!"

"I woke up feeling hungry."

"I brought you a sandwich. Do you think you can eat it?"

"Looks good, thank you."

Milly watched as Marie took a bite of the sandwich. *Thank you, God*. Milly sent up a silent prayer.

"How about something to wash that down?" Milly poured some cranberry juice into a glass.

Marie smiled as she sipped from the glass. "Can you stay for a little visit? I feel so much better, that sandwich was just what I needed. You've done so much for me. I don't know how I'll ever repay you."

"Marie, you're a dear friend, there's nothing to repay. You have a lot of friends that have been praying for you. I'm just the one that is lucky enough to live next door."

* * *

Marie Reader was busy at her sewing machine working on another outfit. She had given herself a Christmas gift of fabric

The Hat Pin Murders

that she was making into a jacket and slacks. She was always happiest when she was at her sewing machine dreaming of a finished outfit. The telephone interrupted her thoughts. "Now who could that be?" she asked the empty room.

"Hello?"

"Ms. Reader, this is Tom at the gate."

"Hello, Tom, how are you?"

"Oh, I'm fine. There's a gentleman here, wanting to see you."

"A gentleman? I'm not expecting anyone."

"He says his name is Jason Williams, an old friend."

Marie gasped and almost dropped the phone. "Jason, did you say Jason Williams?"

"Yes, that's what he said, Jason Williams. Shall I let him in?"

"I'll come down there, Tom, tell him I'll come down there!"

Years had passed since Sandra Malone had seen Jason Williams. So much had happened, nothing was the same. She had lost everything. She had pushed the memory of Jason out of her heart and mind. Now he was here? Was it really Jason, her Jason?

It had been such a long time since she left her home and everything that was important to her. Why would Jason be here now? If it was him. Or was this some cruel joke? Looking in the mirror she wondered if he would recognize her; she was old now. Life had not been kind to her.

* * *

"Jason, is it you? Is it really you?" Marie's heart was pounding. "How did you find me?"

"I read about a Red Hat lady being murdered. My wife was a member of the Red Hats. Those ladies helped her through many painful years dealing with her cancer. I don't know what we would have done without their support."

"Your wife?"

"Yes, Evelyn, she passed away two years ago after a long struggle with breast cancer. After her death I kept finding articles about the Red Hats in newspapers and magazines. The Hat Pin Murder was big news for a while. When I saw a picture of you I knew you were my Sandra Malone. I told my boys all about you and they encouraged me to find you and here I am."

"Your boys?"

"Yes, I have two married sons and three grandchildren. Sandra…"

"I haven't been called Sandra for a long time."

"You didn't seem to want me around, so I married."

"Yes, I remember. I'm glad you went on with your life. I had to take care of Papa. It was best that way."

"I would have helped you, Sandra. I loved you and your father wanted us to get married. We could have worked it out."

"You will have to call me Marie, Marie Reader. That's my legal name."

"I'm sorry, Marie. It must have been awful, your father's death, Carlo Martini, the secret witness program, and then this attempt on your life."

"Yes, but I survived it all. My life was just getting some kind of normality when Carla Martini found me."

"Sandra… Marie, I have all your parents' things. I finally sold the house but I have all the furniture, your father's paintings, even your mother's dishes."

"What? What do you mean you have all my parents' things?" Marie began to tremble. Tears flooded her eyes.

Jason took her hands in his and held them gently. "You know I never stopped loving you."

"I've always loved you, Jason. I was such a fool. My life has been so empty, but I'm happy you have a family. I'm so sorry to hear about Evelyn, I know the heartache of losing someone you love."

"You're still as beautiful as the first time I saw you." Jason laughed. "Remember the day you asked me to go to the car dealership with you? Boy, was I excited."

Marie smiled as she remembered that day and the ones that followed. "Talk about being excited, the day you asked me to go to see *The Phantom of the Opera* I thought I'd die. I couldn't decide what dress to wear and I was scared to death that I'd use the wrong fork at dinner."

"I think we were both nervous. You sure looked beautiful!"

"How did you manage to get all my parents' things? I'd love to see the old house again, but I can't go back to Chicago. The Martini family still lives there and there are too many memories."

"The house and everything in it was sold at auction. I was able to buy it all. I didn't know what happened to you but I knew I had to have all your things. I finally had to sell the house. Some big corporation built high-rise apartments there. I put all your things in storage, all of it."

"They made me leave so fast. One suitcase was all I could take." Marie's body shook, and she cried uncontrollably. Jason held her close to him.

* * *

When Maggie Coppenger retrieved her mail from the box, one item caught her attention immediately. "Frank, look at this!" Maggie's face lit up as she held the invitation for Frank to see.

The honor of your presence is requested

at the wedding of

Marie Reader and Jason Williams

"That's great, that's really great!" Frank said. "After all

these years those two getting back together. Jason is just a great guy."

"Well of course, since he is a classic car nut. You two hit it off from your first meeting," Maggie said.

"I'm happy for Marie, she acts like a teenager in love. It's too bad they lost all those years." Frank wondered how he could survive if he ever lost Maggie.

"Now Marie has a family! Jason has two sons and grandchildren. Can you imagine Marie with grandchildren? She said they are all going to be in the wedding. She's been making flower girl dresses. When she gets that sewing machine going, beautiful fashions just happen."

"She's been alone for so long. I just can't imagine living in fear of being recognized by people that would actually want to kill you. Now she has Jason. He's the kind of guy that will take good care of her. No more being alone," Frank said.

Maggie placed the invitation on the mantel over the fireplace.

"Any ideas about what to give them for a wedding gift?" Frank asked.

"No, I'll check their bridal registry. Milly's giving her a shower. Maybe I'll give her something from Victoria's Secret." Maggie gave Frank a wink and a smile.

Frank put his arms around Maggie's waist and pulled her close, then whispered in her ear. "Sounds like a good idea to me."

About the Author

Joyce has been a member of the Red Hat Society since 2002. She is Queen of her chapter, Noble Babes in Red Hats. She is a proud mother, grandmother, and great-grandmother. She and her husband, George, have been married for 42 years. They lived in California until 1991 when they moved to Cheney, WA. *The Hat Pin Murders* is Joyce's first novel.

Joyce speaks to women's groups, encouraging them to dream the dream that God has placed in their hearts. She is an encouragement to seniors because it is never too late to go after your dream. At 69 years of age, Joyce has published her first novel, fulfilling her lifelong dream to be a writer.